AF418510

The Perfection of the Glass Lemons

R. K. MAYER

To Alessandro

who makes it all possible

This is a work of fiction. Any references to real people, places or historical events are used in a fictitious manner. Any resemblance to actual persons, living or dead, or actual events is purely coincidental.

Copyright © R. K. Mayer, 2017
All rights reserved. No part of this publication may be reproduced, distributed, or transmitted in any form or by any means, including photocopying, recording, or other electronic or mechanical methods, without the prior written permission of the author, except in the case of brief quotations embodied in critical reviews and certain other noncommercial uses permitted by copyright law.

ISBN 978-965-7762-00-4

First published 2017

There is nothing like staying at home for real comfort.

Jane Austen

Emma

I got up this morning with a feeling of dread that I couldn't quite place. I would have dragged myself slowly out of bed, savoring every additional moment of warmth, avoiding the cloud of anxiety that I felt hot and intense over me, but I don't believe in that kind of frivolousness. Once I'm up, I'm up. No lazing or loitering allowed.

I get up and do my regular routine. Breathing exercises: variations on inhalations and exhalations of different speeds and intensities. I do my stretch exercises: not Yoga, of course, too alternative and trendy for my taste. Frivolous. Instead, I do exercises that I have developed over many years of comprehensive Internet research. Hands over face, lean forward and then backwards and then to the sides. Hands behind shoulders, same as before. Hands on hips, same as before. You get the point. Then I start again, doing similar actions, but this time, stimulating my legs and feet. I don't believe in cardio-vascular workout. I believe in keeping blood level constant, heartbeat steady and emotions in check. I have a mat that I unroll for my regular routine. I only get on it once I have sprayed it down with Lysol in order to eliminate any lingering germs and bacteria. Of course, I exercise using gloves so my skin doesn't come in contact with the disinfectant.

From where I do my stretching, I have a full panoramic view of the room. I am surrounded by a sea of white: white walls, white dresser, white closets. My side of the room is spotless and symmetrical to the nth degree: perfectly clean and perfectly aligned – and I like to keep it that way. Jay's side, however, is a complete disaster. Clothes are strewn on the floor. His side table is a mess of used mugs, half-eaten apple cores and coffee-stained coasters. As I begin my morning routine, he is still in bed, but showing definite signs of movement. He usually lets his alarm go at least twice to snooze so that he can prolong his sleep. Today he hits snooze for a third time. Eventually he spills out of the bed, practically rolling out onto the floor. He slides out of his pajamas and into his sports gear that he probably retrieved from under the bed. He says in a sleepy voice, "good morning Emma, my darling, my love," and he comes over to my side of the room to give me a kiss. When he sees that I am in the middle of my meditation, he retreats cautiously, blowing me kisses and stroking the air, as if I have some kind of virtual presence in his embrace. He knows better than to disturb me, because I am really, really trying to get this meditation thing down. I am trying so hard. He continues, whispering, so as not to distract me any further. His whisper is as soft and as gentle as a sonic boom. "Ems, my love, I am off for a jog." He does some stretches and continues, "I wish you would come and jog with me, you would love it." I shake my head like a solemn Buddha and say, "you know I can't do that. Jogging causes sweat." I cannot abide sweat. "Besides which, there are also other joggers," I shudder, "and their sweat is even worse than mine. Now go. I am busy here." I make a face so that he will stop distracting me and I try to settle back into my meditation. I channel butterflies in hayfields and whales thumping their tails in the Atlantic. Jay hasn't left yet; he is doing his pre-jog warmups at home. He is running around the house doing star jumps and flick flacks and for the grand finale, he whips a pillow of the bed, throws it nonchalantly on the floor and dives into a headstand. He balances for around forty-five seconds, head on pillow. I must remember to throw it into the washing machine. When he is done, he dismounts from the upside-down position like a pro, and shouts to me as if I am kilometers away: "I'm headed out my love. I'll bring you coffee," and jogs out of the apartment. All of a sudden there is complete silence in the apartment. The perfect conditions for meditation. But, my time is up. I am on the clock. I have about forty minutes to get ready before he comes back with the coffee. During this time, I put on my disposable gloves, clean up his side of the room, disinfect the sills and countertops and surfaces, and then start the washing machine with the dirty clothes, last night's pajamas and the pillow that he used for his headstand. I make the bed, prepare some breakfast just the way I like it, (hardboiled egg cut into quarters on a bed of lettuce and low-fat white yogurt, and on alternative days: granola and fresh fruit on a bed of low-fat yogurt). I turn on my computer and check out my to do list for today.

I am a freelance Content Writer. I get commissioned to research and write up content for different companies. The topic can be about anything from *Aortic Valve Stenosis* to *Zulu Culture, Past and Present*. I am an excellent Content Writer, because I am thorough, methodological, and prefer not to go out of the house unnecessarily. I am not phobic or anything like that, just very conscious of the perils that exist at every twist and turn in the world around me. I go through my to do list twice. It includes both my professional assignments, as well as my personal tasks and chores.

To do... WORK

SUBJECT	DUE	PRIO	% DONE
Research *Migration Patterns of African Wildebeest*	Today	1	5
Finish article on *Glassblowing throughout the ages*	Today	2	87
Edit paper *How Undergarments Shaped Modern-day Feminism*	Thursday	2	54

To do... HOME

SUBJECT	DUE	PRIO	% DONE
Research vacation in Naples & Amalfi coast	Today	1	0
Price shredding machines	Wednesday	2	0
Call Jackie about Mom	Thursday	2	0
Research *Bombay Surprise* for date night	Next week	3	0

At the top of the "To do... Home" list, my first priority, I have one sentence: *Research vacation in Naples & Amalfi coast.* I give a big sigh, and the feeling of dread rushes back in like a storm cloud. But, I don't have time to dwell on it, because Jay opens the front door and suddenly the room is noisy and busy again. He fills the room like a heavy metal concert. "Hey love," he calls out, "I brought your coffee, babe." He heads to the shower still shouting at me. "Great jog today! Wish you had come with me. Maybe next time? Anyway, will join you in a few minutes." His voice is drowned out by the sound of the shower. I make a mental note to myself to remember to sterilize the surfaces and to clean the bathroom again once he leaves for work.

Minutes later he joins me for breakfast, still wet from his shower, but clean shaven and in clean clothes. There is no way that such a short shower could result in a germ-free body, but this is his one vice, like coffee is mine. I choose to believe him when he says that he is clean and sanitary. When you love someone, sometimes you need to turn a blind eye.

Jay

I met her at the pharmacy. She was buying disposable gloves, sterilizing soap spray, surgical masks and lemon-flavored throat lozenges. She stripped the shelves of the pharmacy bare. I offered to help her when I saw that there were a few boxes left on a higher shelf that she simply couldn't reach. I could tell that she wouldn't leave the pharmacy without them. When I had placed the boxes into her cart, she thanked me for my help. And I told her it was no problem. With the items that she had purchased, I guessed that she was in the medical profession – a doctor, a nurse. Something about her didn't quite add up to caregiver or veterinarian. I guess I made a joke and said something like, *well at least your patients don't need to worry about germs and sanitary conditions when you are around*. She looked at me, paused for a minute and said in a truly authentic voice, "No this is just for me; I like a tidy house." Heavens knows that I am an impulsive person. I am restless and messy and disorganized. I work outdoors as a park ranger, where I can be in the open air, where I can stay active, meet people and breathe deeply. Part of my day is spent with my hands covered in soil, fertilizer and organic waste. I could tell straight away that this was not something that she would have dared to do. She was petite and well-kept. Her clothes were heavily starched, expensively tailored and quite conservative. I was still in my muddy work boots and stained khaki pants. I had leaves and pollen on the shoulders of my uniform and some kind of wet mark, from what – I don't know. My hair was covered with a woolen beany. I was tanned from hours of being out in the sun, and had at least two days' worth of stubble. I towered over her, full of nervous energy and excitement, and the smell of mud. I was absolutely intoxicated by her absolute composure and calm. I think that was when I fell in love with her. To this day, I am not sure what she sees in me. Perhaps I am like a life-long project for her. A thing to shape in her image. Perhaps it's an opposites attract scenario, like some cheesy movie. But it seems to work. We have been together for four years, married for two, but that's a whole other story.

Wherever you go, go with all your heart.

Confucius

Emma

I cannot understand why people want to travel. It is a momentous effort for me to even leave the house. I can't stand shopping, and crowds, and standing and waiting. I can't stand traffic lights and pedestrian crossings and malls. I know it is considered anti-social, maybe even rude, but I can't stand being around people and the noise of rowdiness and jolliness. It's not that I hate happy, but why can't happy be done in private where regular people don't have to see it and be there? Regardless of all of that, I do force myself out the house, because that's what you do when you are in a relationship – you suffer for the greater good. I just *had* to marry a man who is inspired by different places and experiences. Every year it is the same story: he picks the destination and I start dreaming of being killed instantly (or slowly for that matter) in any number of probable or less probable ways. I call them *Death by* scenarios.

Death by the shrill ring of the latest mobile phone that pierces my eardrum and causes my brain to leak.

Death by a squirrel throwing a nut squarely into my eye, shattering it and causing my brain to leak.

Death by a traffic light toppling over and landing on my head, causing my brain to leak.

Brain leakage is the only way that I can see myself getting out of yet another trip. Jay knows that I hate travel, but he thinks it's good for me. He is concerned about my anti-social tendencies. He says travel gets me out the house and into civilization. *Civilization* – as if that actually exists. He is also convinced that it is a matter of time before I grow to love it. "You will thank me in the end, my darling," he says as he runs off to nurse a sick tree, or to check on soil acidity, or whatever. "Eventually, it will happen." I am convinced that *eventually* he will see that he is sorely mistaken.

One thing that I will say for travel is that it certainly shakes up the *status quo*, and rattles the routine. It swings the pendulums wildly from side to side and in doing so, the yearning for balance and equilibrium become even greater. And, once harmony is restored, it is that much sweeter. So I will make the sacrifice and travel for both my husband, and in order to restore the natural order of things, so that life will become more stable than ever it was before. Stability – isn't that what each one of us craves most?

One day this kind of sacrifice will probably get me killed. It is an almost certain, almost definite eventuality. Maybe it will happen this time. Maybe not from brain leakage, but probably from some freak foreign incident that will do me in. Jay will be sorry for a while and then he will find someone else who is not anti-social, but rather more pro-social than me. For me, it will probably be a relief to have died. At least I will never have to travel again. At least I will have some peace and quiet. Jay says that I am becoming more and more like my mother. I completely disagree. She is so negative about everything, and I have quite a sunny disposition. At least when I'm not travelling. Mom doesn't like travelling, but that doesn't prove anything. She says she is uncomfortable in unfamiliar places. Every two weeks, Jay and I go to a different restaurant. I spend a week researching, finding the place, reading reviews, asking questions in the online communities, planning the menu and booking a table. I even look into travel route alternatives, taking into consideration every possible risk, so that we get there in good time. See, every two weeks I go to an unfamiliar place. Not at all like my mother.

Anyway, Jay names the place of our designated destination. Drops it like a glass cup and I am immediately left to pick up the shards, glue them together in such a way that you can fill it with stuff. The phrase "taking a holiday" makes no sense to me. It reeks of inexactitude. You don't *take* holidays; you plan, research, book, travel, pay. If you are lucky, your choices work out and make sense, but it is a whole lot of hard work. Luckily for Jay, my planning is meticulous and thorough and methodological. I practically eat, sleep and breathe the location, doing a full analysis of the area, not only tourist attractions. I also look at economic, cultural and governmental aspects, including of course verifying the details of the local consulate. I do a complete risk assessment of all possible eventualities, as well as potential mitigation plans for these risks. It is stressful and tiring, but someone must do it.

Jay

The world is a fascinating place. I have always felt that way. Life is like a carousel. It goes around quickly. There are a million distractions and a million more stimulants – sounds, lights, colors. Life is teeming everywhere as the world spins around you. I am a restless and curious traveler. I want to go everywhere and do everything. If I happen to settle on the plastic jeep, within seconds I will probably be tempted to mount the bobbing horse or ride the shiny dragon with the orange ray of silicon flame, instead. I want to take it all in. No, I want to *force* it all in. More, more, more. It's like a thirst.

What I see in front of me is never enough. I need to consume that which I cannot see, but that I know of or have heard of or have seen in a fleeting image on some billboard or website. I get an idea of a place to see or a thing to do and *BAM*, I have to do it. Emma calls it the crazies. Sometimes she acknowledges the crazies and gives me a deep soulful look that only she knows how to do. Other times, she looks visibly pained. Then she disappears for hours to her "happy place" and I can hear the whirring of the air purifier, the puffing sound of her inhaler, along with some meditation music: metallic pinging and ponging or shrill bird cries or whale bellowing – whatever that is called. I know that she actually hates those sounds, but is still hoping that eventually they will have some kind of soothing effect on her. Generally, she finds alternative ways to contend with my shenanigans. Like, for instance, about two years ago I went to do some consultancy work in the Blue & John Crow Mountains National Park in Jamaica for about five weeks, and came home with dreadlocks. Emma welcomed me back with a look that suggested that she would like to take a blowtorch to my head. But she didn't go ballistic, or say anything, or even smite me with a raging pillar of fire. She just gave me *the look*. Her patience lasted three days. On the third day, I woke up to find her standing over me wearing disposable gloves and a surgical mask. In her hands she held a pair of scissors that could have cut through glass, and like Delilah, she gently snipped away at my hair. Waking up to your girlfriend of two years holding a blade to your skull can be disconcerting, but she did it out of love and concern for my well-being, or something like that. Frankly, I will admit that it was kind of disgusting and dry anyway – the hair I mean. Let's just say I got the message.

Emma is more of a home body than me. She is happy with her things and her thoughts and her general routine. She has way more structure than me and she enjoys it. She also leverages her love for planning to enrich our lives as a couple. For instance, if there is a new place to eat around town, she looks into it and organizes a date night. She takes care of every tiny detail, from the transportation to the menu. I don't do a thing; she doesn't let me. Kind of romantic really. Her research and planning result in a new experience for the both of us. Our annual vacation is like date night but on a mega scale: poring over maps and weather charts and historical articles for her, and new places and experiences for me. Win-win. That is why we both really look forward to this time of the year when we begin to think about our next vacation. I choose the place and she does the planning, and off we go. Sure she denies enjoying it. Yes, she has the occasional headache, and more than one stress fit before we travel. That is all totally normal. Not everyone can be whimsical and spur of the moment like me. In those rare moments where she's a bit too overdramatic, I have the perfect antidote: I tell her that she reminds me of her mother. A small but powerful punch. A playful trick, but it works.

Emma

We are off to Italy, to the Naples region and the Amalfi coast. For some people, *Naples* conjures up romance, good food, good weather. We'll see about that. I am open-minded and will reserve judgment even though I'm sure that I will hate it and that I will have to spend weeks when I get back, cleaning the layers of dirt off me and sterilizing my clothes.

According to meteorological reports, we need to pack for both sun and potential rain. How absolutely frustrating and inconvenient. I hate inconsistency. I hate layers. On top of that, we also have to travel light. We are going to be on the narrow winding roads of the Amalfi coast. No room for big cars with big luggage. Jay is excited with the prospect of travelling light. I am not overly happy about this. How can I not take my air purifier, disposable gloves, bedding with allergy-free protection, double-thick towels and oil lamp from home? I have packed and unpacked three times. I had an anorak and I took it out. I added a pillow instead. Jay removed the pillow and put in our flip-flops. I am pretty sure that a place that requires flip-flops shouldn't be visited. When the case wouldn't close, Jay removed some more of our things – seven shirts, four pants, and three hats. Thankfully, he didn't come across the oil lamp. He said we don't need to take clothes for the full ten days. We can also buy there. I am gagging at the thought of going into a shop in Italy. It's bad enough to shop here at home.

Jay also said that one hat each is enough. I think he is trying to kill me. Everyone knows that the afternoon sun is hotter than the morning sun. And of course, I need a hat that shields from the wind, because of my sensitive ears. Naturally, I also need a spare hat, just in case I sweat – heaven forbid. I cannot be in a sweaty hat. I am sure it will cause eventual brain leakage. But Jay is insistent that one hat is enough. If I do die from sweaty head syndrome and someone reads these words, I do blame Jay just a little, but I don't want him punished or incarcerated. I am sure that the guilt of directly causing my death will be enough to haunt him for the rest of his life.

I had just finished packing when Mom called and reminded me to take mosquito repellant, antihistamines, antibiotics, probiotics, and a gas mask. I had to unpack again, and recheck the first aid kit. I already had the mosquito repellant and antihistamines (as well as numerous types of gauze, antiseptic creams and some fluoride tablets, but not the other medication). I didn't know what to do because I had no time to make a doctor's appointment to get a new prescription for antibiotics. I was quite distraught. It seemed to me that Jay was pleased with my predicament. He said "Oh no, what a pity," but he had a shiny, smug smile.

After agonizing over the situation for about an hour, I had an amazing brainwave: I began to pack fresh garlic in our luggage. I will chew a clove or two every day to ward off disease and infection. A few weeks ago, I wrote and researched an article about garlic for some medical journal. Now, I will have an opportunity to validate the findings. Jay was no longer smiling. He accused me of potentially becoming a "habitual garlic chewer." This isn't true of course; it is not habitual yet. Anyway, I usually have proper drugs at hand. The garlic is a fallback option only because I have been forced to take matters into my own hand to ensure that I don't come home in a casket. We closed the case. When Jay wasn't looking, I found a Gulf-war era gas mask and tried without luck to push it into the case. I removed three more of Jay's shirts and finally got it in. What a relief. I need to be prepared.

Jay

I am electrified with energy. Emma is lying as still as a plank in bed, and I am pacing around the house – my mind working overtime. We are leaving in the morning, and I am so ready. This is going to be awesome. I am a fly-by-the-seat-of-my-pants kind of person. I have been to way less traditional places than Italy. As far as I am concerned, the further – the better; the more diverse – the more interesting. In fact, I have even been to Italy already, but never to this part of the country. I hear it is spectacular, and the food is great. I don't really care where we stay. I can camp at the side of the road and stay in the same underpants for a week, because that's the kind of person I am. But, I guess that a part of growing up and living with someone is understanding that staying in the same underwear day after day is a no-no. So Emma takes care of those types of things – logistics, lodgings, budgets, inventory – and she tells me what she needs me to execute.

I'll admit, sometimes I relate to her instructions more like recommendations or guidelines, rather than hard-and-fast directives. For instance, when she gives me a list of things to pack, I halve it and then halve it again. I pack my things at the bottom of the case. I do it quickly so she doesn't guess that there are things missing from her list. She has an amazing mind for detail and estimation. She can tell from a pile of clothes in my hands that it is fifty percent less full than it should be. It's one of her many attributes and quite the party trick. She can correctly list what each guest has eaten and drunk, and convert it to calories within seconds. I think this ability is spectacular. Others seem less thrilled. Jealousy? Skepticism? Who knows. On the other hand, when it comes to packing, we do need to travel light and Emma herself needs to adjust ever so slightly. It's not always just about the sheer quantity of stuff; it's also about some of the additional things she puts in there. For instance, there is no real reason to bring thermal underwear to a beach-side vacation. Similarly, there is also no logical explanation whatsoever for bringing an iron to a safari. I pick up our luggage for the hundredth time. It feels good – it has enough weight to feel substantial, but it is not so heavy that it weighs me down. The apartment is cool and silent. I put the luggage down again. Emma needs more things than me. Or, at least, that's what she thinks. I try not to indulge her too much. I did give in on the garlic cloves thing, because frankly it takes no space, and the home remedies that she has learned from her mother or the Internet are like sacred cows that cannot be touched or denied. I learned that the hard way when I refused to cooperate when she tried to relieve me of an ear infection I got from some diving expedition, using onion. Let's just say it was touch and go for a while. Emma can be pretty creative when she's angry with me. She donated all my diving gear – which I actually didn't realize until a few weeks later. She also put onions on my side of the bed, in my coffee, and even, inexplicably, in my shampoo bottle. Maybe it was a bleak reference to the dreadlocks incident. Yet again, I got the message loud and clear. Just tell me this – why do these home remedies all have to involve the likes of garlic cloves and onion? Couldn't the old folks do anything with rose petals and honey?

Perfect numbers like perfect men are very rare.

Descartes

Emma

I am not scared of flying. I know that I am statistically more likely to be killed in a car crash, or die of cancer. I am not sure about the statistics about *Death by* brain leakage. I must do some research on the matter. But, I will be honest, I really hate the whole flying experience. The airport is a germ-infested crowded place. The shops are filled with crowds who are happy to escape from their families and lives, and are in ecstasy to be buying indulgent and frivolous nonsense that they don't need and will never use. They will happily purchase a waffle iron, a jacket with multi-colored beads, yet another three pairs of running shoes, and of course three perfumes for the price of two. In the best case scenario, I can imagine that the multitudes made themselves a waffle in the morning, went to run it off in their new shoes, and then doused themselves with perfume to hide the sweaty smell. The whole scenario makes me want to vomit. I am not sure about the jacket. I cannot begin to imagine who would wear it and under which circumstances.

The airport is another ritual that I can do without. Jay is a stickler for finding the right spot in the Long Term Parking – near the shuttle, but not in the coveted covered spots so as not to draw attention to the car. He's really big on offensive parking, and is extremely reluctant to park facing forward so as to get the luggage in and out of the car with ease. I cannot relate to his absolute insistence on doing things his way. I say, let's park logically so as to make our lives easier. His life really, because I won't touch the luggage while we are in the parking lot. Everyone knows that the air has mold spores and dust germs and toxic engine fumes.

As soon as I get out of the car, I need to hold my breath until the private taxi comes to collect us. There is a public shuttle, but I wouldn't set a foot in that death trap. I am quite the expert at holding my breath. I usually bring a damp cloth that I can breathe into if the taxi is delayed. The damp cloth acts as a natural filter for the inevitable germ-fest lurking in the air. I learned about the damp cloth trick when researching the best ways to avoid smoke inhalation.

Jay is quite exasperating with the parking thing, but I try not to give him too hard a time. I am pleased that he takes his driving role so seriously and conscientiously.

Jay

As I drive to the airport, Emma counts cars. Literally. She has the stamina of a race horse. He counting could put me to sleep if it weren't for her absolute enthusiasm. She counts by the number of passengers in each car. Not by color or type of even roadworthiness of the vehicles on the road. *Four, three, four, two, two, one, two, four, five, one.* Sometimes she adds additional comments under her breath. Words like *carpooling, sustainability* and *carbon monoxide* float around. *One, three, four, three, four, four, two, two, three.* When she gets a sequence of consecutive numbers, either ascending or descending, she literally holds her breath. She likes the order in consecutive numbers.

As we were entering the Long Term Parking at the airport, she was on the verge of breaking her record: *one, two, three, four,* she counted and breathed in sharply. Maybe the next car would score a five? I knew that the moment was critical: if a five should turn up in front of us, it would make our trip. On the other hand, if the sequence was broken by any other number of passengers, Emma might just misconstrue it as a superstitious omen. She denies superstition absolutely, but honestly, she has a quirk or two. Gambling the odds and managing risks is not one of my strong suits, but it took me no time at all to make a decision. I parked in the very first parking space I could find, reversing in quickly before anyone else could take it. Whatever came next would no longer be an issue. A parked car ends the sequence. Emma left the car quickly. I think she was hoping to avoid the feeling of disappointment should there be a sudden arrival of a car with five passengers.

Airports for me are not all that bad. The sequence of various formal encounters – Check In, Security, Passport Control, Duty Free, etc. – is the price we have to pay to get to that elusive place we saw in a magazine or in the Internet or in someone's Facebook post. Sometimes, they can even be enjoyable, if you meet someone new and interesting, or even bump into an old friend.

And you know, sometimes the gods do smile down on you. Our luggage was a manageable suitcase plus an additional carry-on. Parking was immediate; no moving vehicles disrupted the holy sequence of ascending numbers of passengers. The private taxi arrived as scheduled and dropped us at the correct departure lounge. The boarding cards were printed without any issues. I even had time to go off and get us some coffee and bottled water. By the time I got back to the Check In counter, Emma and I were the next in line. There was a lovely lady behind the counter who gave us a great recommendation for a local Neapolitan pastry. I wrote the name down on the back my hand, much to Emma's displeasure. All-in-all, we were out of there in a flash.

To keep oneself safe does not mean to bury oneself.

Lucius Annaeus Seneca

Emma

Usually, I have a number of complaints about the whole Check In scene, but luckily this time the whole process was satisfactorily smooth. Initially, I was certain that we were headed for disaster. Jay went off to get us some coffee, so I was left in line with the luggage. There was a family with four kids in front of me and they were simply taking forever to keep up. The father was lugging two massive old and decrepit suitcases. He had one child body-surfing on top of the bigger case. The mother was carrying the youngest child, a baby, in one of those pouches made from endless pieces of material and she had another little toddler by the hand, as well as two pieces of hand luggage. That left the oldest child, who was around nine years old, to his own devices and mischief. The boy was incessantly fiddling with the makeshift partition. What a hoodlum! If the partitions fall, chaos will ensue and the rational order of movement will break down. To what end does a nine-year-old need to adjust the partitions? Very obnoxious, if you ask me.

It turns out that Airport Security agreed with me, because when I alerted them of this behavior and expressed my concern, the family was whisked away under great protest. Clearly they are guilty of something. Once they cleared out, for some reason the lineup seemed to thin down, or else perhaps the workers finally became more efficient. I would like to believe that I had something to do with that.

Jay made it through to where I was standing just as the lines cleared up. He was beaming to see our lucky position in the line. He reached over and gave me a peck on the cheek and we proceeded together to the Check In counter.

Unlike most others, going through Security is not an issue for me. I enjoy the opportunity to methodologically pack and unpack my hand luggage. I am sure that when the staff see my speed and efficiency, as well as my stellar packing skills, they whisper among themselves how they wish that others could be more like me. I see it as my mission to get through the security gate without beeping. On the dreaded days of air travel, I do a thorough metal and liquid sweep, rid myself of underwire bras, shoes and clothing with any kind of studs or metal lace hoops or embellishments. I never wear a belt, or keep coins, and if I am wearing my glasses, I always select those with extra light, super titanium frames that never get a reaction from the machine. I get rid of my emergency cough syrup and replace it with two kinds of cough lozenges. I reduce my Alco-Gel hand sanitation to the exact milligram limit and distribute my family pack of Dry Eye drops into two separate containers. One stays in my hand luggage, and the other is stored in the first aid kit packed in the suitcase. I could write a book about perfecting the security walkthrough – and maybe I will someday. Surprisingly, so far I have never been commissioned to research it. Jay on the other hand is always spilling over with metal bits. It's like he turns into a human robot. Machines beep and buzz as coins fall out his pockets. He leaves his belt on – *beep*. He has a pen behind his ear – *beep*. His shoes have some hidden metallic clasps – *beep, beep, beep*. I don't want to embarrass him by apologizing to the security staff aloud, but I think they can read my pleading and beseeching eyes, behind the stylish surgical mask that I wear in public places, willing them to forgive Jay in a way that I cannot, because I find his repetitive behavior really frustrating. So instead, as I make it through to the other side, I wipe myself down twice with Alco-Gel (taking into consideration the amount of people who come into contact with this machine daily, it's the very least I can do), and thank each staff member individually, briefly removing my disposable mask just enough to ensure that they can understand me. I then leave Jay to his backward ways and to deal with the hand luggage and the beeping, and I go to wait for him at the passport check, where I stand in line and slowly recover from the embarrassment.

Jay

Emma breezed through Security in two ticks. I took my time and chatted to the people around me. I got a few more recommendations for a night club, a horse riding adventure, and even a wine tasting event scheduled to take place when we are in Naples. Despite the bureaucratic hoops that you need to jump through at the airport, at least it gives one a chance to learn a few things about your destination. Emma learns from research; I like to learn from experience – if it can't be my own, then why not from others? I wrote each tip down on the back of my hands. After getting so much great information, I was running out of space, so some really sweet nine-year-old tore a piece of paper out of the shiny new travel journal that he clearly had no intention to write in and gave me a sheet. His parents looked exhausted, like they were having a really rough day. I guess it's not easy to get through the whole airport ritual with four kids. I was so busy meeting and greeting and writing things down that I almost walked away from Security without my shoes. It would have been really embarrassing to do that again. It is inconceivable to Emma how it happened the first time. To which I always answer the same thing: how often does one get to meet someone travelling with a live snake? I am drawn to that sort of weirdness. Why does he have a snake? Why is he traveling with the snake? Where are they going? Who would possibly approve such a trip and how do you get that approval? Emma is more mainstream I guess. She would rather avoid the snake. Fair enough.

Once Emma and I are together again, we whip through Passport Control. As usual, Emma is a step ahead and is almost at the front of the line by the time I join her. The line that has gathered behind her reluctantly splits in order to let me catch up to her. Within minutes, we are walking though Duty Free to the waiting area. Through the corner of my eye, I see this "Four for the Price of Three" shirt sale. I am usually not really inclined to buy in Duty Free, but Emma has been so awesome in her management of the airport logistics that I am wracked with guilt at having halved my clothes list during the packing process. I point out the sale to Emma, who reminds me that we should travel as light as possible. Right she is, precious swan. I am both relieved to not have to buy anything and at the same time I have a twinge of conscience at my subterfuge during packing. I must remember not to cheat on the clothes list again. We pass a jacket with multi-colored beads. "Hey Emma, this would look great on you," I say. But she just keeps right on walking.

Emma

What a day. There has been so much noise, people who I don't know, people who I don't want to know, and extremely unsterile conditions. People taking off shoes and belts and putting them in boxes in which I place my very own hand bag and scarf. Vomit. I want to just wash the day away, sterilize it in a pool of disinfectant. Jay is like a puppy, running wild, distracted constantly by someone or something, convinced each time that the distraction is willing to play with him. I can't help feeling exhausted for them. They too are here to enjoy their personal space and solitude. When we finally make it through to Duty Free, Jay indicates that he wants to buy four shirts for the price of three. I gently remind him that we need to travel light. So, in the end he doesn't get anything. I thought he would be grateful for the save, but to me he actually seemed quite sulky. I, on the other hand, gave him my shiniest smile of encouragement.

The waiting area is the last stop I remember between our departure from the airport and our arrival in Naples. I vaguely recall sitting on the deep chairs between a nun and a teenage girl with earrings in her eyebrows and chin. I remember adjusting my surgical mask a few times in order to drink the bottled mineral water that Jay bought me. Hydration is imperative. I also remember seeing that family with the four rowdy children again. Then again, maybe it wasn't them. Such is the magic of the wondrous sleeping pill that I brought with me. I drifted from the noisy, smelly, and unsterile airport and was mysteriously transported to another country and place. I recall nothing about the flight, or how I got on it, or made it through. But, I do know that there was no brain leakage. I also know that just as the plane flew up, so it came back down; just like Newton said it would.

Jay

I love her, I really do. But, I still remember the incident on the flight to Turkey. I also cannot forget her hysterics on the flight from Zanzibar. There are the stories or urban myths or actual truths about the germs and the stale air that circulate in the cabin. There are the passengers who cough and sneeze incessantly and those who take off their shoes first thing. Heaven forbid she should need the toilet. Heaven forbid anyone sitting next to us should need the toilet. We have been travel companions for longer than we have been in a married, committed relationship. So yes, I did slip her an extra sleeping pill.

By prevailing over all obstacles and distractions,
one may unfailingly arrive at his chosen goal or destination.

Christopher Columbus

Emma

A few hours later, we found ourselves in a little white rental car. When I say little, I mean tiny, practically microscopic. When Jay first saw it, he beamed from ear to ear. When he sat down in the driver's seat and realized that he would be driving more or less with his knees next to his ears, his enthusiasm dropped about four of five notches. After four attempts to put our luggage in the car, Jay eventually found the correct angle and we were off. The roads to the hotel were impetuous and insolent. They did not seem to align with the GPS guru who spoke to us in an annoyingly calm voice as he led us in the wrong direction. Perhaps, that luminescent voice was actually purposefully trying to steer us off course. To what end. I don't know. A warning? A prediction? A technical glitch? Jay nonchalantly steered us through the dark streets while I cursed the GPS gods and the Italian urban planners. Miraculously, we arrived unharmed at our hotel. I am generally not a vindictive person, bar that time in the ice cream parlor where I got the server fired for serving vanilla swirl and coffee pecan with the same spoon. But this time, vindictiveness got the better of me. When I got out of the shiny white car, I gave it a swift kick in the front wheel. If Jay says the car is so smart, then it will get the message.

Jay

Emma woke up completely at the car rental place. She was kind of sleep-walking before that. Sleep-walking is not actually a bad state for her. She's like a serene ceramic goddess – all glassy-eyed and zombie-like. When we went through Passport Control, she didn't even register when the on-duty officer licked his fingers to turn the pages of her passport. Usually something like that would totally set her off. She didn't comment when I accidently shoved her into a travelling soccer team of teenage boys. Actually, they also didn't seem to mind. She also didn't really seem to mind that I seated her next to a toddler eating a peanut butter sandwich and wiping his grubby, little fingers on the seat next to her, as I went to gather our luggage from the revolving conveyor. Once I retrieved our case, it was kind of hard for me to shepherd her forward and to lug the baggage at the same time. So, initially I tried to support her with one arm and balance our things with the other, but that was kind of awkward, because the carry-on bag kept on falling. Then I tried to move her forward a couple of meters, leaving her sitting on a bench, if there was one, or leaned up against a pillar of sorts, propped against one of those insulated smoking cubes or balanced next to one of the mineral water vending machines. As she waited, all balanced and dazed, I went back for the cases, moved them forward as far as possible and then went back to fetch her. That's how we made it to the rental place. When we got there, I sat her down with the luggage while I got the car. In a straight line, it is probably about two hundred meters to the car rental. I estimate that it took us about forty-five minutes to get there. But who's complaining? I have my serene dove by my side, we are in glorious Italy – what more could I ask for? I like to try new things whenever I can. I was more or less sweet talked into renting one of the smallest cars that I have ever seen or been in. The car agent promised me an experience, and he wasn't wrong. He told me that the car was perfect for the narrow winding roads of the Amalfi coast and that I would be like one of the locals. He painted a pretty romantic picture, but I must admit that my first impression as I sat down was that this is not quite the experience that I was looking for. But by that time, Emma was fully awake and I thought it better that we hit the road and head to the hotel. I know that things have a way of working out for the best. Emma was rested, the car was ready, and I had walked up and down juggling between a dazed Emma and our luggage that my body was completely loose and pliable. I felt inherently capable of driving with my chin knocking against my knees, even if it was something that I was not absolutely sold on doing. So I loaded the car. Then I offloaded and reloaded it another three times so that Emma could have the full peripheral view, as she prefers. Once she was satisfied and I was satisfied that she was satisfied, we drove off.

The ride was smooth and seamless. I was so enchanted by the mysterious night sounds, the road signs in exotic Italian and the promise of the sea in the distance, that I barely listened to the deep voice of the GPS calling instructions from the soul of the car. I just drove as if led by a secret hand. My angel with bright eyes, Emma, chose our hotel, researched the location and set the GPS. But that evening, as I drove with Emma by my side, it was like a magnet drew us to our destination. Either that, or we were simply led by the stars.

Every step of life shows much caution is required.

Johann Wolfgang von Goethe

Emma

Our first few days were to be spent around the coast of Naples in the hotel that I had selected. The hotel boasted both a pool and direct access to the beach. When we arrived at eleven p.m. sharp, all I can tell you is that it looked dark and dreary and nothing like the shiny pictures on the Internet. I made a mental note to myself to contact the one hundred and eighty-three people who ranked the hotel highly and point out the inaccuracy of their ratings and shame them for their fraudulent feedback, should this turn out to be the case.

I braced myself for the worst when I noticed that the reception had glass fruit on display. Why? To what end? Glass fruit is one of my very few pet peeves. Glass fruit, balloons, blue eyeliner… Jay flinched when he saw the shiny glass grapes. He looked at me and I could tell that he was begging me with his eyes not to pick a fight with the animated receptionist who was so eager to welcome us to the establishment. Given the fact that I had already promised to never again violate glass fruit displays after the shopping mall incident two years ago, I put a few drops of Rescue Remedy under my tongue and went to sit down and wait for Jay to get the key to the room. Within fifteen minutes, we were checked in, and settling into our hotel room. We were both exhausted, but after an international flight, two airports, a taxi and a rental car, there is of course no other choice but to shower. As usual, Jay somehow manages to do this in six minutes flat. Let me reiterate, I don't mean to question his hygiene at all, but is it really possible to be completely clean after less than a quarter of an hour of cleansing? He says that this is one of the fundamental differences between him and me. I would like to believe that he is correct, but unfortunately, in my heart I know that he couldn't possibly be.

I must admit the shower wasn't bad. Lots of hot water, a heavy stream, a hand shower-head with easy access, and at least five to six paces between the sink and the toilet. The amount of germs that waft from the toilet to the sink boggles the mind, and makes me want to vomit every time I think of the toilet germs that I am inhaling as I brush my teeth. After so many years of being together, Jay understands my needs, so ahead of time he ordered six extra towels and special organic soap with no paraben. Shampoo made from olive oil and carrots, more disposable gloves – just in case I run out of what I have brought – and ammonium spray so that I can clean the bathroom myself before first use. After just one hour and fifteen minutes, Jay and I were both in bed. Probably sleeping but maybe not. It's hard to say with absolute certainty.

Jay

Once I parked our tiny chariot, I squeezed myself out the driver's seat, and did a couple of jumping jacks to loosen my legs after the slightly cramped but wholly intimate drive. I then took our luggage from the back of the car, sliding it out quite easily from its tight spot, and headed briskly towards the reception. Emma also did a couple of stretches as she got out of the car. No doubt her neck was sore from trying to follow all the street signs. On the way out, she banged her foot against the side of the car. Poor dove, that must have hurt. It has been a long and hard night for her. I guess she is still suffering a bit from the aftereffects of our airport jaunt, and maybe perhaps some delirium from the sleeping pills. We arrived at the grand entrance of the hotel. It was dramatic and dark and the way was mostly lit by delicate fairy lights. It looks amazing; my precious queen has outdone herself. We were greeted at the reception by a young lady, Lucia, who sat behind a rather large centerpiece of glass fruit. It turns out that she is working at the hotel in order to put herself through college, where she is studying landscaping. We have a lot in common, Lucia and me. I am a park ranger and a lover of the great outdoors. She is a landscape artist with an infinite love of nature. We spoke about her wish to run her own tree sculpting business and she showed me some pictures of her babies – bushes and trees sculpted in different images: a garden gnome, Olaf from Frozen, and of course some of the religious iconography that you see around here so much. So enlightening and inspired and whimsical. What a talent she has. I suggested that she use Emma as a muse. Not that I would like to share my wife of course, but great things of wonder cannot be hidden.

As Emma sat on the leather sofa in the reception waiting to go to our room, I spoke of her fine attributes to Lucia. I explained that Emma's greatness has a price. She is beautiful and intelligent, but she is also quite delicate and sensitive to certain things. "For instance," I said to Lucia, pointing to the center piece of the reception, "this glass fruit, to you and me, fills the space with happiness and light. But to Emma it represents something frivolous. You cannot touch it or use it. This center piece has no artistic, or historical, or religious significance. It can't be eaten; it is purely decorative."

Lucia nodded, although I am not absolutely sure that she understood what I was trying to say. Emma is passionate about this issue, but her passion can be a bit too zealous and the last time she tried to remove a glass fruit display from a shop window in our local shopping mall, we ended up needing to pay a rather hefty sum for the destruction of private property. To this day, Emma remains unrepentant. She didn't care about the money. One less glass pineapple was her gift to humanity, as far as she was concerned, she said to me after the incident.

Where do you get that kind of commitment and passion nowadays? She is a shining beacon to us all. "Just to be clear," I said to Lucia, "when you see us coming, please cover the display." Lucia nodded again. "I think I understand" she said. "For us who work with nature, we would never choose to have plastic flowers in our home." I nod with satisfaction at the comparison.

Lucia and I continued to discuss a few more things we needed to do to keep Emma satisfied. When Emma and I first started to travel together, I began to compile what was a couple of notes, and is now a minor pamphlet. It contains roughly seventeen requests that are wholly doable. At least most of them are. Banning certain items is harder to request. Glass fruit can be hidden from sight, but the unexpected appearance of talking parrots or visiting clowns is harder to predict. The items in the pamphlet that are relevant to Lucia relate to basic dietary issues, bedding, sanitation and, of course, code of conduct. They affect most of the staff who will come into contact with Emma during her stay. Isn't it great when someone knows exactly what they want? I am always searching and craving for something new. Emma is always crystal clear and absolutely certain of her needs – what a breath of fresh air!

Lucia was a gem. Among certain people, this list triggers a bit of eye rolling and shoulder shrugging. Not Lucia – she was patient and tolerant and understanding. I can see why she would be good with plants. She has a very gentle and nurturing approach.

When befriended, remember it; when you befriend, forget it.

Benjamin Franklin

Emma

Jay woke up like an excited puppy. He marveled at the room, the sheets, the bed, the pillow, the view from the window of the pool and the coast, and in the not-so-far distance, the majestic Mount Vesuvius. He breathed in the fresh air coming from the shiny blue-green waters of the clear sea, did some wild acrobatics, stretches and one of his regular headstands. As he was perched upside down, he announced to me that he was ready for the day, so the day better be ready for him. I have always admired his enthusiasm; it is a bit like watching a glass of soda gush over. If my sunny disposition is bright, his is luminous; practically nuclear.

I put on my darkest sunglasses, took a deep puff from my inhaler and three and a half drops of Rescue Remedy, homeopathic liquid and braced myself to leave the room. The Rescue Remedy was quite fortuitous, because the first warning sign of the day was loud and clear: *Death by* elevator plummet. Under no circumstances can I imagine that it is acceptable for fifteen people to squeeze together in an elevator. I mean, between the collective weight of the crowd and the collective germs and bacteria that they give off, there is an unlimited number of risks to be mitigated. I make every effort not to touch the handrails or the elevator buttons. It is a balancing act, but not something I haven't practiced on many occasions in preparation for just this kind of scenario. By the time we made it into the breakfast hall, an excited Jay had made friends with a German family, a Danish couple and a group of Chinese tourists. I staggered out and took in the oxygen that I had denied myself for two and a half floors. While I was in the elevator, of course, I did deep breathing exercises so as not to keel over from lack of oxygen, but I did them as discreetly as possible. I am quite sure that the others were not able to discern from my composure that I was holding my breath. This is one of the things that health conscious people need to do in order to maintain equilibrium. Jay the Magnificent was off like a rocket and within minutes, he had got the head waiter, Carlo, to prepare us both cappuccino (caffeine, my one vice) and had ordered eggs, in a special way, just like I like them: hardboiled and cut into quarters and on a bed of lettuce with low-fat white yogurt. Initially, I walked behind him, willing him quietly to restrain himself, and listening carefully to ensure that he didn't make plans with any of these new-found acquaintances. I walked with sophisticated composure behind him, scarf partially covering my face, as he galloped like an over-eager puppy from person to person. I am glad that Jay is anthropologically intellectual and curious, but I am not able to bear interlopers when I am trying so hard to avoid potential brain leakage situations. The German toddler was playing with his toys with his chocolatey fingers. I suppose his mother allowed him a pre-breakfast indulgence. The Chinese tourists wanted to take a picture with me posing just outside the reception desk next to a new receptionist whom we hadn't yet met. Jay saw the murder in my eyes. He looked from the glass fruit decoration at the reception to the excited group of tourists, made a quick and accurate calculation, and adeptly steered the tourists into the breakfast hall and towards the Danish couple instead. As he went to order specially prepared coffee and freshly squeezed juice, I went to find us a nice secluded table, far, far away from everyone else. Within minutes, the table was laden with food, coffee and sweet-smelling orange juice. Jay joined me. He sat himself down and stretched out his long legs. He looked so relaxed and at ease. The view from our table was truly marvelous. The combination of the Italian bay and the majestic volcano in the near distance was breathtaking. It was on the tip of my tongue to thank Jay for insisting that we come to this place. With the others around us completely blotted out, Jay and I enjoyed a moment of serene bliss and calm. Feeling the good vibrations and Zen, he took my hand and said with a sigh: "Isn't it great to be here? Isn't it soulful and beautiful and inspiring?" I nodded and remembered the many reasons that I love him. His romantic gestures, his floppy hair and big eyes. "This place, so intense and yet so volatile."

I nodded, wondering slightly how the word *volatile* had slipped in there. What could he possibly mean? Jay continued: "Just imagine the sights that we would see if there were to be a sudden breach of this tremendous quiet. Just imagine the tranquility that would come to a standstill should Vesuvius erupt in all her glory at this very moment."

I am not sure what happened next, but when I came to, my shirt neck was damp with freshly squeezed orange juice, I had a taste of black cherry jam in my mouth and I had yogurt and egg on my forehead. The Chinese group were standing over me. The Danish couple and German family were politely trying not to stare, the waitress was kneeling two tables away holding one of my shoes and Jay was tapping me incessantly on my shoulder.

With the last bit of my drained energy and with as much composure as I could muster, I hissed at Jay. "What do you mean the volcano is active?"

Jay

I awake to the rocking of the waves and the distant smell of sea spray. Emma is already awake and doing her morning health regime, and her regular attempts at meditation. What a world, what a place, what a day! I am simply ready to conquer it all with my special lady by my side. "It is going to be a wonderful day. I can feel it in my bones." I announce to Emma and I spring out of bed.

I always begin my day with stretching and flexing and a brief cardiovascular workout that includes running on the spot, crab walking, and side stepping at varied speeds and gaits. I also do various types of kicks, depending on my mood. The workout always ends with me balancing on my head, letting the juices flow from the tips of my toes to the depths of my brain. Oh invigoration and spirit, this is the life. Emma tries not to watch me, because sweating unnerves her and I tend to sweat a lot. Besides which, it distracts her from her routine. While her ideal wakeup routine is slow but sure, mine is baptism by fire. She is the calm and I am the storm. But at some point, when we are both showered and ready. We leave the room and there are no polar extremes, just an equatorial bliss. We go hand in hand to the elevator and everything is just perfect. The elevator stops for us without even having to give a press of the button. The doors slide open. In the elevator is a simply charming family, a young German couple and their toddler.

"*Guten Morgen,*" they say in chorus.

"Good morning" I say, and Emma nods. Conversation ensues and within seconds we are all introduced.

"Hey buddy," I say to the little one. "What have you got there…?" In his little hands he has a battery-operated red firetruck with a remote control, and a Spiderman figurine. His mom bends down to him:

"*Der Mann fragt, was du in deinen Händen hast?*" – the man is asking what you have in your hands." The tot just giggles and hides behind his mom.

"He is a bit shy," the mother says.

The elevator stops again and another couple gets in. They are laughing and giggling and you can just tell that they are here on their honeymoon.

"Good morning! I am Jay and this is Emma, and this lovely family is from Berlin and they are Jürgen, Frauke and Timo – and Spiderman. The family waves and hellos are exchanged all around.

"What a fascinating place." I say.

"Indeed," says Jürgen.

"*Ja,*" says Frauke.

The Danish couple look at each other and giggle.

"So, how is the breakfast here?" I ask.

"Oh, unbelievable," say the Danish couple. "You should try the grapes!" the girl says and the couple giggles again.

"I guess I will then," I say.

"There is something for everyone, here, thank goodness," says Frauke. "Timo is a bit fussy."

"Have you all been to Mount Vesuvius yet? We can't wait to go," I say.

"*Ja, ja,* we've been." say Frauke and Jürgen, "What an experience, so great. And the hike was easy, even for Timo."

"Well, we were going to go," says the young Danish man, "the name is Anders by the way, and this is Klara. It is on our agenda, but we haven't quite gotten round to it." He and Klara laugh.

"Say no more, there are children in the elevator," I say to them, and then everybody laughs. Emma gives a precious half smile. She is still and regal, like a statue. She is also kind of quiet like a statue too, except for a tiny whistling sound.

"Well, we have been spending some time on the beach as well," Klara adds. "It's not like we are locked in the room all the time," she says and blushes.

"Oh, *Ja,*" says Jürgen, and laughs at the two of them. "The beach is amazing. We don't have that in Berlin."

The elevator stops again, and the doors open onto a group of about eight Chinese tourists.

"All aboard!" I shout, and we all flatten up in order to let them in. Emma flinches ever so slightly and I can hear her inhale deeply, but I am sensitive to her quirks and hygiene sensibilities, so I make an invisible barricade between her and the others so that her personal space isn't invaded.

The tourists are from Shanghai and I quickly ascertain that this is their first time in Italy. They pull out the camera and we all do an elevator selfie. The Germans, Danes, Chinese, and me and my lovely Emma.

By the time the elevator opens, we are like old friends. I steer us quickly through reception, noting that the glass fruit is proudly on display again. For a brief second, I consider sitting near our new friends so that we can exchange travel tips and ideas, but Emma, ever the romantic, breaks away sharply and finds a table as far away and as intimate as possible, so we can enjoy the time, just me and her. As she glides away towards the table of her choice, overlooking the bay and beneath the formidable silhouette of Vesuvius on the other side of the bay, I go up to the head waiter to order our coffees. After I introduce myself, Carlo, the head waiter, knows exactly who I am and what he needs to prepare for my sensitive swan. I can see that the lovely Lucia has really assimilated my instructions pamphlet and passed it on as requested. Carlo sends for Emma's pre-ordered breakfast spread and it reaches our table even before I do. How wonderful when things work out as planned. I saunter over to Emma with two glasses of freshly squeezed orange juice. I place the glasses on the table between the freshly cut flowers and the freshly baked pastries, and I sit down. I reach for Emma's hand and together we take in the exquisite surroundings. My heart is overflowing with the newness of everything and the overwhelming sense of endless opportunity. At that table, by the shimmering sea, under the watchful eye of Vesuvius, I share my thoughts with my Emma.

*The secret of realizing the greatest fruitfulness
and the greatest enjoyment of existence is: to live dangerously! Build your
cities on the slopes of Vesuvius!*

Friedrich Nietzche

Emma

Jay led me back to the room. It is more accurate to say that he carried me, because of my severely weakened state and the fact that I had only one shoe on. I made a mental note to myself to chew an extra clove of garlic and to take an extra dose of my inhaler should I make it back to the room. At the ding of the elevator, I lifted my unshod foot even higher so as to minimize all contact with the elevator floor. I inhaled deeply, so as to not breathe in any micro germs and spores. Elevators are no different from public toilets in terms of the germs they amass. Jay seemed to slump a bit in the elevator under my weight. I am not sure why. I weighed no more than I weighed the previous night, given that I hadn't had any breakfast yet and I had one shoe less. He's a strong man. He has felled trees bigger than me. He should be able to manage to balance me, my shoe and one glass of freshly squeezed orange juice. I said to myself: *To the powers that be, if I am going to die, don't let it be now. Don't let Vesuvius erupt when I am half shoeless and in a closed casket of death hanging between the second and third floor of this Neapolitan hotel.*

With a ding, the elevator opened and within a minute we were back in the room.

After a fifteen-minute power nap, I still feel sapped of any energy. I wearily pulled myself up to an upright position. "What do you mean the Volcano is active?" I said to Jay. I could tell that Jay himself was nervous. His face was white and he was fiddling with all those ridiculous pamphlets that the hotel leaves in the room:

spa with hot rocks, aromatherapy, wine tasting workshops. Whoever makes up that nonsense? Have people nothing better to do?

"I thought you knew, honey. That doesn't mean that it will erupt, now or today or tomorrow or even this month," he said in a breathy voice. "It just means that we should be aware."

"Aware of what, that we will be toasted and fried? Mummified and petrified? This is worse than being in a room filled with glass fruit *and* balloons *and* circus clowns with blue eye liner." I hate clowns. "Way worse."

"Honey, you can get past this. You are strong and vital, and when you climb the mountain you will see that it can be done."

"When I climb the – what – climb Vesuvius? Have you lost your mind? What else do you have in mind, shark diving without a cage? Bungee jumping without a rope?" I swooned dramatically back into the bed and pulled the covers over my head. Jay came to the edge of the bed and kneeled. He put his hand on my leg. I could feel it through the sheets. "Honey, you can do this. Thousands have done it before you. We won't go today. Today we will relax at the hotel and you will build up your strength. You can do this, Honey."

I slipped down to the very bottom of the bed, praying that the mattress and sheets were sterilized since the last guest. Is this what brain leakage feels like? Like the world is a hammer on your head and someone keeps calling you honey?

Jay

As I pace up and down in our hotel room, I try to keep the noise levels down. Emma is still for now, but I can practically feel the tension, like an angry cloud of hot smoke, emanating from where she is lying under the covers. This is a first. I can't believe it. I truly can't believe it. The basis for our relationship is open communication – not agreement and consensus.

Heaven knows that Emma and I are different in many ways. We have different opinions, needs, triggers and reactions. But Emma is the researcher, the oracle, the planner, the ultimate know-it-all – in the nicest possible way, of course. If I do happen to agree with her a lot, it is simply because she is always right. It is mind-blowing to me that this is the one fact that she missed. Doesn't everybody know that Vesuvius is a live volcano? That fact certainly hasn't stopped hundreds and thousands – no, millions – of people from building their homes in the surrounding areas. It certainly hasn't stopped the steady swell of tourists. Well, there is nothing to do about that now. We are here and this is going to be an amazing vacation and that is a fact. I nod to myself, pleased with my unilateral decision. Emma lets out a low moan. I am not sure whether it is one of her far eastern meditation techniques, or whether it comes from a deeper place in her fragile psyche, as she recalls this morning's events. Notwithstanding my optimistic decision that we *will* have fun and enjoy our vacation, Emma's dramatic faint and dive into her breakfast, must really have hurt. Physically, I mean. Not to mention the obvious ego bruising that such a public spectacle causes. It is probably a good thing that she doesn't know about the whole finger incident. Upon seeing her collapse, Changming, one of the Chinese group that we met in the elevator, came charging over. After a few seconds of assessing the situation, he stuck his finger in the jam and then thrust it into Emma's mouth. "Sugar," he said, "she need sugar." I probably won't tell Emma about that. She is a bit sensitive about other people's fingers in her mouth. Thanks to Changming, Emma came to quite quickly. I grabbed the freshly squeezed orange juice to go, took Emma's shoe back from that waitress, who had grabbed it from little Timo.

Timo, first on the scene, had carefully balanced the shoe on his red fire-truck, filled it to the brim with sugar sachets and was driving it off towards his parent's table. I took the orange juice and the shoe and carried them both to the slowly recovering, but still basically comatose Emma. Little Timo started to cry at the injustice of the shoe being whipped away so abruptly.

"Sorry, little buddy," I called out. "Sorry folks," I yelled, hoping that Jürgen and Frauke would hear. Finally, I swooped in and picked up Emma and started to make my way back to the elevator.

We passed Lucia at the reception on the way to the elevator. She saw us and hastily covered the glass fruit display. "*Signor* Jay, is the *Signora* OK? You need help? A doctor?"

"No, no, we will be fine." I said. "*Buongiorno!*" Lucia answered. "Have fun then." I trudged over to the elevator with my three passengers in tow: Emma, the orange juice and the lone shoe. I wish I could say that this was a first time that I was in such a situation. But, as I stood there waiting for the elevator, I remembered that incident in the restaurant back home. We were in this fancy new place that Emma had discovered. There was a string band playing classical music, and the waiters wore gloves. We were sitting at a table by the back of the room, when a rat brushed up against Emma's foot. I never actually saw it, but Emma swears that it happened, and if the commotion is anything to go by, she meant it. Her anguish was genuine. I hauled her out of there, but left her shoes and part of the sleeve of her pants suit that she hacked off with a steak knife because it had been touched by the rodent, at the restaurant. *At least,* I thought to myself as the elevator doors opened, *at least this time she remained fully clothed.* That's not to say that the balancing act was so easy. At a certain point, Emma accidently kicked my knee and my legs buckled momentarily. It took me a few seconds to regain my balance. Despite being a whole night after our car ride, I admit that I am still a bit stiff from the journey in that tiny, white rental contraption. Nevertheless, we finally made it back to the room. I deposited her in the bed, and helped her to take some home-made emergency resuscitation measures. Bless her, she is amazing. She always knows exactly what to do. Although, I do wish she would find an alternative to the garlic.

There are moments when it is important to realize that a person is teetering on the brink. Emma is really strong, and I was positive that in time, she would come around. But this was a real setback for her, and like Mount Vesuvius – the situation was volatile. So, weighing my options and considering very carefully how to deal with the situation, I left her lying in bed for a few minutes and I stepped out of the room. This situation definitely required the heavy artillery, so I whipped out my mobile phone, found the group selfie from the elevator and punched in a quick caption: "Missing you…" Gave it another few seconds of thought and then added "lotzzz." The caption now read, "Missing you lotzzz," and I sent it on – to Emma's mother.

Water is the driving force of all nature.

Leonardo da Vinci

Emma

About two hours later, I found Jay lazing by the side of the pool. Or rather, lazing at one of the three pools. There was a pool for infants and toddlers, covered with bamboo and palm leaves. Another pool was for dipping and moving about lazily, for those who prefer quiet and solitude. And there was a larger pool for more active swimming and, hopefully, no water games or splashing children. Not that children don't have rights too, but there should always be clear boundaries. I am always on the lookout at swimming pools. The first sign of the entertainment crew and that is my cue to exit. Too much happiness and foolhardiness. If we were meant to dance in water, we would have been born with webbed feet and fins. At the first sign of beach balls and – heaven forbid – frisbees, I am off, without looking back for a second.

Jay reached over and gave me a big hug. He said nothing about Vesuvius, although it was literally directly in our view. He asked me nothing about my mood or my health or my potentially leaking brain. He was perfectly composed, absolutely calm, and totally Zen. Pure Jay.

"So how's your mom?" he asked. I unfolded my arms and dropped them loosely by my side. Jay worked out years ago that when my arms are tightly folded, it's a sign of maternal intervention. He calls it my "fetal position."

"She's fine," I said gruffly. "Can you lather me up?" I asked, changing the subject, and handing him the sun cream. Jay gave a little smile and started to lather the cream in, making circular motions on my back and shoulders.

Some moments after Jay had left the room, after I had chewed an extra garlic clove hoping for rapid recovery, taken my inhaler, drunk my freshly squeezed orange juice, tossed and turned in bed, and attempted a transcendental meditation while listening to an eleven-minute clip of dolphins and whales, the phone rang. Still not thinking clearly, I made the mistake of answering it straight away.

"Emmy, where are you?" she asked in a panic.

"I'm in Italy, Mom. You know that," I answered.

"You didn't call or write to let me know that you had arrived. Here I am, waiting for a sign, anything – and not even so much as a pigeon brought a message for me. With all the evil in the world, I worry about you." she said.

"I'm fine, Mom. Jay and I are here. Nothing is wrong. We are OK and having a wonderful time."

"Jay!" she mumbled and then muttered something about grammar. I couldn't quite hear. But then again, I was still a bit unsettled. I walked over to the balcony and stepped outside. I was suddenly overwhelmed by a gust of fresh air, the smell of jasmine, lemon blossoms and sea salt. The sea glistened like a bed of emeralds and diamonds. I felt a deep yearning to be enveloped by the crystal clear water. Up ahead, Vesuvius winked at me in the distance.

"The plane could have gone down, or worse, you could have caught a nasty disease from all the filthy germs circulating. The rental car could have stopped working on the highway. The hotel could be an absolute dump. You could get food poisoning from the foreign things they eat. Have you even examined their kitchen or interviewed their chef?"

Thankfully, there was no mention of active volcanic eruptions and dying in a sea of molten lava. Does Jay really think that this active volcano story is such common knowledge?

"But none of those things happened, Mom. Everything is good. I am good. Italy is good. There is no need to worry or to be negative."

And it really was. I could do this. I am a positive person with a sunny disposition. I can do this. I don't want negativity and nerves. I will do this.

"Mom, all is well, I promise I will drop a line regularly. I promise." I reassure her.

After a bit more chit chat and once I could hear that her breathing was regular and constant, I blew my Mom a kiss over the phone and hung up.

I can do this, I thought. *Damn you, Vesuvius.* I raised my fist to the mountain and shook it. *Damn you!*

I thought back on the conversation as I sat by the side of the pool with Jay, wondering how to help my mother overcome her nervous anxiety. *It must be debilitating,* I thought, *to be so highly-strung.* Jay lay drip drying on the recliner seat. I moved my chair slightly away from him. Even the smell of chlorine makes my skin break out. I sat next to him in a big lazy chair, covered by the spare sheet I took from the room, wearing an oversized towel robe that I procured from the highly sanitary spa on the way down to the pool. I loosened my floppy hat and took it off and put my sunglasses on the side table next to the chair. I pulled the sun roof way over my head so I was completely shielded from the sun. *You can't be too careful,* I thought to myself.

Jay

Emma is a great planner. She believes in the thirty-to-seventy percent approach to vacationing: seventy percent of Rest and Relaxation or the big *R-and-R*, and thirty percent of planned and well-researched activities. Our vacation is around ten days long. Ten days away from the regular day-to-day hustle-and-bustle. With that in mind, the agenda consists of several pre-planned and sometimes pre-booked main activities and the rest of the time is all about hanging around at the beach and the pool, eating well, lazing, reading, and of course, regularly scheduled sex. Needless to say, a visit to Pompeii and Vesuvius is in the cards; it always was. But, after Emma's recent epiphany, it is hard to know where we stand on that, and I know that she needs a bit of time and space. She will eventually come around. I am positive about that. If she wants time and space, I can give her both. We both swim a lot and Ems practices meditation whenever she can. One evening, she relaxes on the balcony in order to practice some deep breathing under the Italian starry sky and I meet up with Changming and his friends at the bar. We spend a wonderful evening talking about Western versus Eastern culture, playing cards and, of course drinking. He teaches me some Chinese phrases, or at least so he claims. The laughter from the group was a bit too suspicious.

Changming and the group are having a wonderful time in these parts and will be moving on soon to Rome. It turns out that he drives an ambulance and has had some paramedic training. He tells me that he has exchanged his ambulance in Shanghai for a bright yellow minivan while he is in Italy. "Driving through the streets of Italy is like I drive to accident. Lots of cars, people shouting and shaking their fists," he says, "I feel right at home."

One early morning, I get the crazies. I feel absolutely compelled to take my exercise regime out to the lawn by the pool. As I am doing flick flacks and jumping jacks and stretches, an audience gathers, including Frauke and Jürgen and little Timo, and even Lucia from reception, who is on the grounds shaping a nearby fern into an elegant seashell. I end up giving some basic instructions for doing headstands. I have a captivated, if not very coordinated group. Lots of spilling and laughter ensues. Frauke is relatively limber and makes several valiant attempts to follow my instructions. Jürgen is determined but seemingly incapable of having his feet off the ground. His loving wife does what she can to balance him and hold him up. But she is no match for his height and weight and they tumble over, stopping short of crushing little Timo. Having given up on her husband, Frauke encourages Timo to get in on the action. But headstands are hard to achieve when one of the hands, which is meant to be a pillar of support, is surreptitiously being led by the finger to search for hidden treasures in one's nose. Em watches from the corner of her eye, vaguely involved in her own repose. But when the crowd gets a bit too boisterous and the laughter gets a bit too raucous, and just when Timo begins to have more than moderate success with his nose digging, I see her slinking away towards the serenity of the pebbled beach. She is on a whole other level of calm.

Emma

Bear with me for a second because I am about to wax lyrical. These waters are clear waters, bejeweled with ripples of azure and aquamarine. Cool currents flow and retreat, and warm currents intermingle with gentle foam and soft bubbles of air. My olfactory senses are heightened and clear. My ears ring with the rise and the fall of the water swells. There is nothing more perfect than the sea.

On the other hand, pools are the chlorinated illusions of relaxation and repose. They are actually bodies of toxic hazard. I never swim in pools unless I can do a detox shower immediately afterwards.

As anyone who knows me knows, I am fairly germ conscious. I am proactive in both openly criticizing and avoiding those who pollute or vandalize public areas, and in welcoming and executing a healthy, body-mind regiment. I do this in order to encourage and maintain stellar health.

Being on vacation naturally disrupts my regiment of regular inhalations, stretches and flexes. It curtails my regular ammonium sterilizations of all entry points – windows, sinks, doorways, keyholes… – and Kirby vacuuming every other day. We are generally at home before we miss the monthly fumigation. And luckily, we have never yet skipped the yearly home detox. Most people have some sort of regular routine. I do one or two extras, because of my super-vigilant nature. But, if I am forced to leave this rather stringent routine, the sea presents an impressive alternative. Water deep enough to stretch and flex and move around in, and all this while being enveloped in salt, one of nature's most efficient cleansers. Jay is amused at my enthusiasm. Sometimes he raises an eyebrow and I can tell that it is on the tip of his tongue to point out the many ways in which I am deluding myself about the absolute cleanliness of the sea. But I am calm and collected when I am in the water. I think even Jay can appreciate that. So I glide like a water nymph in the waters that are bluer than blue, and both cool and warm at the same time. And for those moments, the world is mine and the world is me. Even if Vesuvius is laughing at me and mocking me, overhead, every time I raise my head above the water.

Jay

Two days at the hotel and we haven't yet stepped out into the city of Naples. So on the morning of the third day I am up like a firecracker ready to go. I bounce off the walls as I do my morning exercises. I am so excited. While it has been fantastic to be at the hotel, I am aching to do something different.

Emma, with her usual calm and composure, is doing her own routine. Somehow, it seems much longer today, which is probably only due to my own anticipation and excitement. Today she is doing breathing exercises combined with what looks like breast stroke. I have never seen her to it before. She is doing this exercise over and over again. After her morning regimen, it takes her even longer to pack her travel handbag with her regular supplies as well as some extras that she thinks she needs because we are spending the day away from the hotel.

"Jay," she says sweetly, although I detect a note of annoyance in her voice. "Do you realize that you are tapping your feet on the edge of the bed? It is distracting me."

"Sorry, my love," I say, "it is the excitement of getting out. I feel like a caged tiger about to be set free."

"I understand, but unfortunately, if you don't stop, I will definitely have a migraine. I can feel one creeping in."

Poor love, migraine is one of her ailments. I think they may stem from her really deep thinking and analytical skills. Her migraines do tend to happen at key moments of change.

"My bird of peace, what can I do to make it easier for you?" I ask.

"Just give me a few minutes to fully concentrate while I get my things in order," she says. After a pause, she continues, "why don't you wait for me at the reception? Go find out if Lucia has some tips for us," she suggests.

"Good, good, great," I say and grab all the things that I need, (peaked cap, keys, wallet) and leave the room.

Naples is the flower of paradise. The last adventure of my life.

Alexandre Dumas

Emma

So, we have this jam-packed itinerary. I simply hate the word jam-packed, it sounds gooey and sticky and sickly sweet. We have this really comprehensive itinerary. Of course, the agenda is of my doing. We have had two days of strict relaxation, to level the adrenalin and to restore homeostasis after intense air travel. Now that that is done, it is time to trigger the senses with some external stimuli. Jay sees it as another amazing adventure; I see it as a necessary evil when it comes to travel. In order to achieve physical and emotional balance, one needs to swing the pendulums to over-activity. Therefore, this will be a day filled with triggers and stimuli, just like Jay likes it: lights, sounds, people, and a lot of movement. To prepare, I do my morning regimen extra slowly. I once more fail to meditate, but I do manage to add some precautionary drills: inviting the oxygen to envelop me like a protective aura. Jay looks like he's about to jump out the window. He has so much nervous energy. Today, I find his excitement to be debilitating and distracting; usually, I am much more amenable. I am watching him from the corner of my eye, even though I am meant to be detoxing my aura. I still need to pack my handbag. I also need to somehow slip the oil lamp in, and I don't really want Jay to see it, given the fact that he has explicitly asked me not to take it. Not that I need his permission or anything, but you know, sometimes, he is unaware of the extent to which I am dedicated to keeping my mind and body healthy. I am simply more holistic than most, and the oil lamp is calling out to be brought along. I take a deep breath and say:

"You are tapping your feet on the edge of the bed. It is distracting me." Indeed, his tapping is like Chinese water torture.

"Sorry, my love," says Jay, "it is the excitement of getting out." I know he means this. He needs to get out in order to recharge his batteries.

"I understand, but unfortunately, if you don't stop, I will definitely have a migraine. I can feel one creeping in." I make a pained face. Jay is Superman, but when I have a migraine, he flies off in a pinch.

"My darling, what can I do to help you?" Jay says. Feeling just a twinge of guilty conscience, I turn to him and say, "please give me a few minutes alone to get my things in order." And "why don't you wait for me at the reception? Go find out if Lucia has some tips for us."

"Good, good, great!" says Jay and out he gallops out of the room, noticeably happier.

So I kick him out of the room and ease the oil lamp into my bag.

Jay

At Lucia's recommendation, we leave our little rental at the hotel and take a taxi into the heart of the city. Jürgen, who took a car into the city, landed up parking in an illegal place, and got a heavy fine, heartily agreed with her. Carlo the waiter, who has now become a steadfast friend and an expert at getting just the right temperature and the right amount of foam into Emma's cappuccino in the morning, doesn't really understand why tourists insist on cars anyway. Why, when mopeds and scooters are so much easier to maneuver? I have so much energy that I feel I could probably run there, but Emma, like a dignified stork, doesn't glide that quickly and hates to perspire.

We have an intense day planned, from eating in one of the several pizza restaurants that claim to be the oldest in the world (my idea) to walking in the underground tunnels (also my idea) to exploring a few cathedrals and museums in order to get an infusion of culture and history.

Emma is not big on crowds or shops, so today will be a bit of an ordeal for her: navigating, walking, being out-and-about. But that is what I am here for – to be her human shield.

I love Naples from the minute we step out of the taxi and into *centro storico*, the historic center of the city. "We will see you later," I yell to Giorgio the cab driver, who has agreed to bring us back to the hotel at the end of our busy day, "*Grazie!*" Giorgio has also told me which restaurants to avoid and which side streets to stay on, in order to not get lost. At least, I think that is what he told me. Frankly, he was quite difficult to understand. He may have said the exact opposite and maybe he won't be back to fetch us at all (that is Emma's theory). But who cares – we are here and breathing in the life of the city. Narrow, cobbled streets are lined with modest-sized buildings with high ceilings and inspiring edifices.

"If these buildings could tell stories," I say, "we could be here for months."

"If these buildings could tell stories, Emma says, "they would say *run away*." Emma is already a bit tense.

"Ems, look at the architecture, look at the streets, so narrow, just imagine how hard it must be to deliver the mail, or to collect the garbage."

"I can just imagine. Apparently it is impossible," she says, eyeing a sizeable amount of trash at the side of the road.

"If you see that now, imagine what it must have been like hundreds of years ago, when they didn't have the means and the technology that we have today." I tell her. "And if that is hard to imagine, then just imagine that you are in a time warp. You are a beautiful, young Italian woman. You have walked from your neighborhood to come and clean the house of a rich gentleman. You are tired when you arrive and he offers you a glass of white wine, and…"

"Jay," Emma says, panicked… "not now" – she looks around her, flushed and nervous – "not here." I guess I must have set off another trigger.

"OK," I grin and make a mental note to remember to finish off what I have started.

Art is not what you see, but what you make others see.

Edgar Degas

Emma

Before stepping into the taxi, my surgical mask was already carefully in place. Taxis house way more germs than elevator buttons, but definitely less than buses. Jay was chatting with the driver as he is wont to do. I have no idea what they were talking about, although Jay seemed to think that he did. My planning and mapping of things to do doesn't include researching and learning common key phrases in local languages. That would entail me actually talking to people, and that falls into Jay's jurisdiction, as it were. But since Jay is more hands-on and less studious than me, he doesn't see the need to focus on actually learning new expressions. He inherently believes that he can make himself understood, and that he can understand others, by sheer will power. He also believes that all humans have common body language and inherent instincts to help one another. I have told him that this is hogwash. Body language isn't universally common, and people don't have instincts of good will. I know this because my body language is frequently misunderstood: otherwise, why would anyone ever imagine that I would actually be interested in having a conversation with a complete stranger? As for the need to instinctively help, what can I say? If this is true, then my kind of help is to stand back and let others step in. Too many cooks spoil the broth.

But here we are on the garbage-lined streets of Naples, with the smell of cigarettes and textiles in the air. Romantic? – not so much. Impressive? – perhaps. But boy, would I like to take a bottle of ammonia and rub the place down. I would need extra-strength double-thick disposable gloves, of course. I try to touch nothing and to let nothing touch me. Not such an easy situation given the oil lamp that I am lugging around. There are crowds and crowds of people around. Who knows what diseases, germs and foreign particles they bring with them. I know that Jay is watching out for Changming and his group. But there are bus loads here with passengers from all over the world: large and small, young and old. There are performers, buskers and street artists that I avoid at all costs. There are North Africans selling fake merchandise. I feel myself walking closer and closer to Jay. There is the sound of violins and opera singers, police sirens and ambulances. There are smells of pizzas, baked and fried, cheeses and wines, citrus fruit in drinks, in wreaths and in salads. There are smells of perfumes and leather, plastic and feathers. There are gelato shops selling ice cream in a thousand colors and flavors. There are bakeries with cakes and pastries that I have never seen before, but whose smell I can practically taste. Jay is holding my hand quite tightly.

There are vendors selling jewelry and clothing and soccer gear and toilet paper with pictures and sayings. There are little stands selling religious charms, rosaries and bracelets. Jay has his arm around my shoulder. There are old buildings, ancient paths, arches: a city that has many treasures in and around it. Finally, everywhere there are beautiful statues rising from the cement: lions and horses, archangels, apostles and saints, and the Madonna and Jesus, all welcoming the guests with open arms. In all that noise and hustle and bustle, I stop in my tracks. We are in *San Domenico Maggiore* square and towering above me is an obelisk with a statue of the Immaculate Virgin. She stands regally, a marble vision frozen in town, watching over the crowds from above. Protected from the noise and mess and commotion, she reigns above the daily struggles and challenges taking place here in the street. I would love to be a statue. So calm, so solid, watching the world and seeing it with the eyes of someone who has seen everything and has the wisdom of the timeless. Someone with eternal balance who is not in a never-ending race against time to find inner peace.

Jay

It's easy to be caught up in the throngs and to follow the crowd. If it were just me, all by myself, I would probably just ride with the tide and see where it takes me. But Emma has other ideas. We step into several cathedrals and museums of her choice. We don't stay there for hours. Sometimes we are in and out in a matter of minutes. For each place, she has mapped out exactly what she wants to see and why. She paints a tale of a historic Naples. She tells of generations of art, politics and power. She talks facts and figures and intimate details about who built, who designed, who commissioned, why, what and when. She talks dryly and at length and yet she is genuinely awed by this thing that she has come to see. Her eyes are open wide as she talks, and she talks in a breathy manner, like she is in a race against time to share. Of course, she has impeccable taste and an eye for detail, but this is also a kind of purge for her to let out all the things that she has bottled up inside. I am amazed by how much she knows.

I am game for any adventure, and honestly, I don't really care whether the spectacle is a fresco in *Duomo di San Gennaro* or a decorated and painted elephant in Thailand. I am here for the rush – not for the thing itself. I am here for the bigger picture and the action that produces it. Today that rush comes from watching Emma. When she stops at an object, and begins to talk, the people around her stretch and crane and try to listen. But she just steps nearer to me and speaks a notch softer. She is like a work of art herself, my Emma.

Emma

Jay has had an intense morning. I have kept him busy going from place to place. All the research that I have done so painstakingly on the city of Naples is gushing and pouring out like an overrunning cup; it just spills and spills and spills. I like to spin a good yarn and I do get myself a bit lost in the tale.

We must be a funny pair: him tall with a floral shirt, Bermuda shorts, a non-descript peaked hat and a pair of rough looking boots, listening intently to me: a short and petite lady, formally dressed, as if I am out on a safari, armed with a surgical mask and wide-brimmed white straw hat over tightly pulled back hair, lugging a large leather handbag. But there you have it. I guess there are stranger couples than us around here. In fact, there are throngs of them. But it is now lunch time and we have come to eat at one of the several restaurants claiming to be the oldest pizza establishment in Italy. Because there are disputes around the authenticity of these claims, my choice for lunch settles on which place appears to be the most sanitary. I personally vet these things, and it always begins in the same place: in the bathroom of the restaurant. My theory is if the bathroom is clean, the kitchen is likely to be clean. I have been to establishments that look spic and span on the outside. But, on examination of the lavatories, I have felt the need to gag and retch. After the bathroom, I take a look at the waiters. Are they gloved? Do they have visible tattoos or piercings? Are they touchy feely with one another? Do they swing in and out needlessly from the kitchen? Finally, I check out the menu: if it is laminated, has it been wiped down? If it hasn't been laminated, in what state is it? In what languages is it written? Word to the wise: if there are more than two languages, I will generally not stay. This is an indication that the place caters to the lowest common denominator (with an emphasis on *common*). Finally, and really not trivial at all:

if the menu is written in English, I check for language and spelling. I cannot tolerate poorly conceived menus. I was once a guest in a particular establishment where carp was misspelt as *crap* – a self-fulfilling prophecy if there ever was one. Maybe one day I will write a book about restaurant inspection. I am sure that it will be a bestseller.

After thorough inspections, we take a seat in the third place on my list, a restaurant that meets my criteria in the most satisfactory manner. We sit and eat a pizza that is both tasty and simple. Not ostentatious, not over embellished, just right.

Jay

Emma is exhausted, but I am exhilarated and have boundless energy. I lead her to the first restaurant on her list. She usually has several options, just in case she discovers that one of them does not meet her standards. This does have a tendency to be the case somehow, since we almost never stay at the first place that we enter. Nevertheless, I will say this for Emma: she doesn't tarry or dawdle. As soon as she finds a fatal flaw, we are out so quickly that it seldom becomes embarrassing. She doesn't kick up a fuss or demand to see the manager to point out the obvious issues. She doesn't leave a signed note with contact details, just in case the establishment requires more information. Generally, she just gives me a look to say *we are so out of here*. If there are diners, she looks at them with disdain and/or pity and we leave in a flash. Of course back home, this would not be the case, because then Emma feels responsible to share the information that she has with others. She feels it is her obligation, because that is the kind of giving person that she is.

At the third place on her list, we finally take a seat and I take over the ordering for both of us. I order pizza margarita, red wine and San Pellegrino, as well as a few of the fried vegetables that are so popular here, for starters. Emma has her hat pulled low and her sunglasses on. She seems to have forgotten that she has them on. I would normally give her a little nudge, just because I know how important correct etiquette is to her, but I can see two of the waiters arm-wrestling behind the bar. They are huffing and puffing and working up a sweat. This is definitely the time for ignorance to remain blissful.

Emma

My energy is up again, and we are headed towards the Naples underground city. This is one of the most curious things that I discovered when researching at home. It is not the most curious thing that I *didn't* discover – I still cannot believe that I somehow missed the fact that Vesuvius is an active volcano – but the dreaded mount is out of sight at this precise moment in time. The downside of this little underground adventure is that it is marketed as a family and children-friendly venture, as well as a rainy-day activity, so I have mapped this day out for when it is *not* meant to be raining.

Hopefully most of the families will be at the beach today. I am preparing myself for the worst experience, the ultimate punishment. How can any guide possibly assimilate and impart two thousand years of history – from the Greeks to the Romans and up to World War II – within the dusty excavations of this rough-and-tumble, unpolished city underground?

The probability of calamity is extremely high, but I have analyzed it thoroughly and done some significant risk mitigation planning. The main scenarios on my latest *Death by* list include:

Death by collapse of the tunnel. In this case I will use the emergency exits that I have thoroughly researched.

Death by oxygen deprivation. I will light my oil lamp and use it to ascertain oxygen levels. Should the flame die out, I will use emergency exits and can be out in a matter of seconds.

Death by dust balls and other microscopic germs. None of the sites I scoured has a spore count or a dust outlook, so to be on the safe side, I took a double dose of antihistamines last night. Of course, I also have my surgical mask on to protect me. I did offer an additional one to Jay, but he prefers to rough it.

Death by rust. After all, the tunnels were once used as a massive garbage chute and there are still some relics left behind of old ammunition, toys, and vehicles. Who's to say that one couldn't by some freak accident rub up against something like that? Well, thankfully my tetanus is still up to date. I made a point of checking that out, twice.

Death by slipping from the moisture. In this case, the best mitigation plan that I can think of is to stay near to Jay so that either he will block my fall, or else he will pick me up if necessary. If he slips first, however, that is a completely different issue. Also, if someone else gets stuck between the narrow pillars, I guess we will all need to starve ourselves until that person can squeeze his or her way out. I have made a mental note to stand between Jay and a person with a relatively slight physique.

Finally, should there be an earthquake or should an *unnamed* active volcano erupt and spill lava into the nooks and crevices, well, I will not live to blame Jay forever. That will probably be the most infuriating scenario of them all.

Jay

I have been looking forward to the subterranean tunnels – *Napoli Sotterranea*. It sounds so different to what we have done up until now, a world within a world, below the world. I heard that it's quite the workout: an hour underground with no daylight, and weird moisture and precipitation in the air. You traipse through narrow tunnels and hallways and climb up and down very steep staircases. I have been practicing crab-walking so that I will be able to navigate the narrow paths with ease.

There are times when being tall or large is not ideal. I am pretty sure that this is one of those times.

We have just arrived at the entrance to the tunnels, having just finished our pizza lunch. It has occurred to me that squeezing through tight corners would have been preferable on an empty stomach. However, on the other hand, after such a sumptuous meal, it is going to be really great to have a good workout. We are in *Piazza San Gaetano* waiting for the next English speaking tour to begin. A crowd is gathering, all ready to begin the expedition, and among them we see our friends Changming and company. They come up to us, happy and excited. They are all wearing the bright blue T-shirts of SSC Napoli, the regional soccer team. They are munching away on gelato and *sfogliatelle*, a sweet warm cheesy pastry. I have already eaten two of them today.

"Hello all!" I say.

Hello, *nǐ hǎo*, hello. Hello, *nǐ hǎo*, hellos are shared all around.

"Hello Emma," says Changming delicately. She is standing near the group, but not with us, a vision of serenity and beauty. I have another vision: one of Changming's finger encrusted with black cherry jam in Emma's mouth. I try to block it out. I am unable to even look at Emma. I have a wave of guilt for not telling her.

Emma walks over to Changming and the rest of the group and says "hello." She gives them all a modest nod from beneath her massive white straw hat. She has a look that says to me that she is calculating something in her head. Sometimes she does that. Today, she counted how many pizzas were eaten during our lunch at the restaurant. She worked out how many pizzas were shared and how many were eaten by single individuals. She also noted how many people entered the restaurant to eat, but did not order pizza. I am not sure what she will do with this information, but I am sure that someday she will recite these facts as she has observed them. In any event, she turns to me with an animation that is quite unusual for her. "Jay," she says, "I think that we should walk with Changming and the group." The surprise must have registered on my face, but Emma just gives a sweet smile. "Sure," I say, "absolutely!" Changming is thrilled. He translates the good news to the rest of the group, who cheer and chatter away in Mandarin. As the Chinese-Napoli team cheered for Emma, their enthusiasm must have been contagious, because from around us, we hear spontaneous calls of *"Forza Napoli"* – "Go Napoli!" from some of the locals walking by. I guess they made quite an impression, the Chinese-Naples soccer team.

We gather together, the last people to join the English speaking group. Together we walk into the narrow hallway that leads us down and away into another world, away from the light of day.

Thousands of candles can be lighted from a single candle,
and the life of the candle will not be shortened.
Happiness never decreases by being shared.

Buddha

Emma

I have a brief moment of internal debate before I step into the dark underworld. I have the *Death by* list flashing through my mind, but I also have my current mantra ringing loud and clear that to obtain equilibrium, one must first upset the pendulums. I remind myself of the Pro... list that I created to counter the *Death by* scenarios. Clearly less dramatic and final, but significant nevertheless: down in the subterranean underworld, there are fewer people, fewer crowds, less noise, less traffic, less commotion, less pollution, less distraction, and the temperature and weather are both regulated and stable. As for darkness, well, sometimes it can be a welcome friend. As I am in the final throes of deliberation, my cell phone pings and I pick up the message from the corner of my eye. The message is from Mom. It says: *I just read that thousands of tourists die every year in foreign countries. I have a bad feeling about Italy. My arthritis is particularly severe today and this is clearly a sign. Come home.* I steel myself, take a deep inhalation from my pump, and step into the darkness, placing myself firmly behind Changming and in front of Jay, hands folded in front of my chest.

Lorenzo is our guide. I make sure to listen very closely to him, which is not easy considering that there is English-Chinese simultaneous translation going on right in front of me. It feels a bit like a mosquito is in my ear. But I need to do fact checking and to validate how comprehensive my research of this place has been, and maybe send a comment or two back to my Web information source. So far, Lorenzo seems to be doing a fairly good job. I have a list of subjects that I expect him to cover and I give him the occasional nod of approval when I am able to check the topic off the virtual list in my head. There are others on the tour who are not English speakers: a group from Holland, a family from Israel and a few students from a variety of other places. But language does not seem to be an issue. What does affect some of the underground travelers are the actual conditions. Some people just don't belong in confined and dark spaces and these few are already showing signs of distress and claustrophobia. There are others who can get along anywhere, but have attention deficit so intense that they fiddle and fidget around, distracting everyone else on the tour. Twenty-five minutes into the tour and there are already four people who choose to head out and leave the tunnels. The mother of the Israeli family leaves with the youngest of the three children, as he won't stop crying. Perhaps he is scared of the dark? Maybe he thinks this dark underworld is haunted? Who knows what is going on in his little mind? The mother apologizes profusely for disrupting the group. Jay offers her his sympathy. "No matter," he tells her, "he's just a little kid." And turning to the little one, he says, "don't you feel like you are in Batman's cave?" Whether the kid understood or not is unclear, but he did begin to cry even more hysterically. In addition, one of the Chinese Napoli soccer team Bao-Gabbiadini, who feels like he cannot breathe as we go deeper and deeper into the Earth, backs out apologetically, wheezing and coughing, clearly stress induced. Insigne-Changming volunteers to go with him, but Bao-Gabbiadini waves him off. The last casualty backs out after we have been through several winding tunnels, past the botanical university experiments and the underground art installation, and just before we get to the narrowest part of the leg of the underground journey. She is part of the Dutch group and is easily two meters tall and quite overweight. With the encouragement of her friends, she chooses to sit it out.

Lorenzo gets us ready for the narrow passage. "Keep your bags in front of you, and/or walk sideways *come un granchio* – like a crab." Jay gives a big thumb up. "Breathe" he says, "*non dimenticare* – don't forget to breathe, it is not a long way to walk, but we cannot turn back. We cannot turn around, so if one person gets stuck, so does everybody else." The group looks around, sizing the remaining travelers up and down for girth.

"Up until now we have used electricity to light the way. But from now, we continue in the dark." There is a nervous outbreak of comments in low undertones. "But don't worry," says Lorenzo, "we will hand out candles, you know, we make it *romantico*." There is a relieved sigh and a giggle from the group. "But, not everyone will get the candles," he continues, "because there are not enough to go around." The earlier relief turns once again into nervous consternation. This is my moment to shine, quite literally. I pull the oil lamp out of my handbag and prepare to light it up.

Jay

Emma is simply a goddess. I know I asked her not to take that lamp, but here we are in the dark, not enough light to go around, and she pulls a rabbit out of a hat. We have already started edging through the narrow pathway. The walls tower above us. I walk on my side. I can feel the cool stone against my back. If I walk too quickly, which really isn't possible, my forehead bumps against the wall in front of me. When I look up, I see the wall, but I can't really look up because my head is at an awkward angle. I am the last in the line. Emma is in front of me. I can't see her, but I can see the light of the oil lamp and I can hear her counting: *five, ten, fifteen, twenty, twenty-five...* she counts slowly and methodologically in multiples of five. For the most part there isn't silence but rather a dull undercurrent of chatter – smatterings of Chinese, English, Hebrew, and Dutch.

This place is an unlikely womb and the passage that we take is an awkward and challenging birth canal. *Fifty, fifty-five, sixty, sixty-five, seventy,* Emma chants. I wonder whether she can see Changming in front of her. We edge forward, step by step. For once, Emma is quicker than me. She has more agility and speed in this small space. She remains a step or two ahead of me as we journey forth. Each time she edges forward, for a brief second in time, the light weakens and fades. Quite unexpectedly, I feel my pulse accelerate. But this is as fast as I can go, so I try to enjoy the solitude and not to think about how limited the space is around me. For a few brief moments, the line stops moving. I can hear nervous giggles. A tall young woman with a scarf around her neck, from the Dutch group, has dropped her bag and can't get to the right angle to pick it up. Her boyfriend, just ahead of her, instead of easing her through and directing her to a solution, teases her and chooses to immortalize the moment of her duress with the camera of his mobile phone. They will definitely look back at this moment and laugh, but for the rest of us, our rhythm has been broken.

"*Kom op* – come on already," their friends urge them on, "*we wachten* – we are waiting," and "*Hou op gek te doen* – stop messing around." Mumbling from the Chinese group becomes louder, and the kids from the Israeli family start to jabber away too. Emma moves on from multiples of five to a more complex round of citing from the periodic table: *Argon, Arsenic, Astatine, Barium…* I think to myself: *this is what it must feel like to be between a rock and a hard place.* To say that everything is OK, would be lying. At this moment, the walls definitely seem to be closing in on me. The world seems to be getting darker and further away. My breathing begins to feel tighter and tighter. I fight the urge to panic or bolt, both of which will only make the situation worse. I feel heavy. My body feels hot and sticky and prickly with tension. Maybe I will melt. Maybe I will explode. Then all of a sudden, like a voice from the heavens, I hear Lorenzo sing:

"Che bella cosa è na jurnata 'e sole…"

The sound carries clear and bright. It envelopes the group like a warm pillar of light. From the first person to the very last, a collective breath is loudly inhaled and slowly exhaled. From the oldest to the youngest, the glorious sound lifts us up and unravels us from whatever knotted tension we may have been experiencing in that dark, restricted space. Emma's chanting halts and I hear her whisper, one word, "yes." I close my eyes and lose myself in the moment. Lorenzo's voice comforts and restores me. The wave of panic subsides as his voices gets stronger. *"'O sole, 'o sole mio, sta nfronte a te, sta nfronte a te!"*

Lorenzo's voice crescendos and I think of how claustrophobia is no match for the power of song.

How ironic that in that dark tunnel, in that narrow space, in that moment of hesitation and turmoil, a Neapolitan song celebrating the glorious Italian sun should pull us through. Like a wave released to the sea, the group suddenly becomes unstuck and those who can't sing, whistle. Those who can't whistle, hum. Those who can't hum, count: *four hundred and fifty, four hundred and fifty-five, four hundred and sixty, four hundred and sixty-five, four hundred and seventy.*

Emma

The narrow path opens up to a chamber in which there is a clear pool of water. The purest water there is. I regret that we are in this space, contaminating the air and spreading our germs, because it really feels like a sanctuary. It feels like hallowed ground and that we are intruders or plunderers. I can see that the others too are in awe, or maybe they are simply relieved to finally be standing upright. But, I want to leave as quickly as I can, to leave as small a footprint as possible in this beautiful, unspoiled well. "It's time to leave," I announce to Lorenzo, breaking the silence. "Yes, indeed – *è vero*," he says and shepherds us out, already beginning to talk about the next leg of our journey through time. *Seven hundred and five, seven hundred and ten, seven hundred and fifteen, seven hundred and twenty, seven hundred and twenty-five* – I hold my breath as I count. We are walking through hundreds of years of history in the blink of an eye. *Seven hundred and thirty, seven hundred and thirty-five, seven hundred and forty, seven hundred and forty-five*: who will be counting for us in a thousand years' time?

Jay

Naples is still ringing in my ears. I am reluctant to leave, but the day is done. From the museums to the churches and ending with the Neapolitan underworld: the narrow tunnels and passageways, the Roman theater, which turned out to be housed behind the trapdoor of the sitting room of a regular local family. We have definitely seen a lot. Emma, my history goddess, is completely spent. We sit and wait for Giorgio to pick us up in his taxi. Truth is that I am not one hundred percent sure we are at the right place. I am also not one hundred percent sure that this is the time that we set to be collected but Emma is post-inhalation and mid-meditation, and we are sitting in a little bar in *Piazza Bellini*, drinking an espresso and sharing a chocolate *baba*. Actually, Emma is sitting and I am wandering around, stretching my legs and appreciating the Italian sun from above Earth's surface, as opposed to from down below.

The piazza is relatively tame in comparison to some of the other places we have been today, but nevertheless there are a few people mulling around. I talk to a professor and her husband, who have just been in the nearby Archeological Museum. I talk to a group of local students, who are bored and nonchalant and are more interested in hearing more about where we have come from than to talk about the city in which they are living. I stop to speak to a group of four girlfriends who are celebrating their fortieth birthday year in Italy and seem to be spending their time getting partially abrasive and completely drunk. They summon me over as I am pacing up and down.

"Hey you," says Woman One. "You're cute. Come here."

"He's not cute; he reminds me of Richard, that bastard," says Woman Two, "fuck Richard."

"Fuck Richard," says the chorus of women and down a shot.

"Fuck Richard," I say, and raise my hand in a mock toast.

"Yeah!" they cheer.

"Come here," says Woman One again. "Whatcha doing here? Are you getting drunk like us?"

"I don't think so," I say. "I'm here with my gorgeous wife, that amazing creature over there," and point over to Emma who is practicing meditation, seated on the bar stool and doing breathing exercises, her hat pulled tightly over her eyes.

"Crap," says Woman One. "What a cliché, all the good ones are taken, or gay. Are you gay?"

"Why's she got that mask?" says Woman Two, pointing at Emma. "Is she sick?"

"Shut up, Liz," says Woman Three. "That's not very polite of you to ask. He will tell us only if he wants to… so are you?"

She bats her eyelids at me.

"Am I what?" I ask.

"Is she?" asks Woman One.

"Is she what?" I ask.

"Gay," says Woman Three. "Sick," says Woman One at the same time. Both of them have completely forgotten that some questions are considered to be impolite.

"I am not gay and she's not sick; she's just... cautious." I explain.

"Oh, one of those," says Woman Four. "Fuck cautious," she says to the group "and fuck Richard!" she yells out not-so-delicately.

"Yeah!" cheer the other not-so-gentle ladies.

"Fuck cautious!" Woman Four yells again, this time directed at Emma.

"What's her name, love?" Woman Three asks me.

"Emma," I say, not sure why I am cooperating with these women. "Her name is Emma."

"Emma, take off the mask," Woman Three yells again. "Fuck cautious!"

As the chorus of "fuck cautious" resonates from the drunken forty year olds, from another corner of the piazza another sound begins to build. It sounds like a grating mix of carnival music and heavy furniture being dragged. A group of street performing clowns are entering the square. Emma hates clowns, maybe even more than she hates glass fruit. Between the heckling of the rowdy women and the cacophony of the travelling carnival, Emma's meditation was now completely ruined. No longer able to concentrate, Emma lifts her hat off her eyes. She spots the clowns at the same time I do. As the accompanying music of the marching clowns gets louder and louder, so do the acrobatics and antics multiply. I am torn between a desire to get Emma out of the piazza and an impulse to run and join the street artists in their street gymnastics.

From where we are situated, we can see the performers and their heavy makeup, bright clothes, and accompanying props. Stilts, balloons and whips are gradually getting nearer and nearer. Emma, her meditation deep freeze unthawed within seconds, starts flinging sugar sachets at them. The packets aren't heavy enough to reach anywhere near them. In fact, it is unlikely that the clowns even noticed. However, my new-found friends – the drunken ladies – inspired by Emma, also begin to fling sugar packets towards the street performers. When they run out sugar – white, brown, and dietetic – they quickly graduate to salt and pepper, and then move on to napkins. Liz even reaches inside her handbag and starts throwing tampons. Woman Three, not to be outdone, flings tic-tacs and Woman One simply stands up and catapults her whole bag over her shoulder. The music gets louder and louder, but so do the ladies. Emma is now poised for full-on frontal attack, and from where I am standing, I am pretty sure that the next thing that will be thrown is the oil lamp. I start running towards her, preparing to block the oil lamp in mid-flight, to throw myself on it, as if it were a grenade. "Emma, wait," I yell. Within three strides, I am in front of her and blocking her pitching arm.

Just as Emma is about to throw the oil lamp, a bright yellow minivan pulls up, tires screeching so loud you can smell the burning rubber. It stops right in front of the bar, and the driver's window and the side door are thrust open with a very loud clang.

The driver hangs out from the car window. He is wearing a bright blue Napoli SSC shirt. "Emma, Jay, we thought it was you. We go back to the hotel; we have room for you. You want to join us? Just hop in." It's Changming and the Chino-Napoli soccer team. I look at him with a mixture of disbelief and overwhelming gratitude – the ambulance driver made it to the scene, even before the accident could actually take place.

Emma is paralyzed and petrified in position, the oil lamp locked and loaded, ready to be blasted off if not for my block and Changming's save. The drunken ladies are still yelling and the clowns are getting nearer and nearer.

"How can I? How can I get into that minivan?" Emma mumbles to herself. "Just imagine the germs and diseases lurking in there. Can you imagine the number of people who have been in there and sat in those seats?" I can visibly see her shudder and shiver. I think that I can see her gulp back some saliva. Now is definitely not the time to tell her about Changming's finger in her mouth. "Fuck cautious, Emma," I say firmly and hustle her inside the vehicle.

Emma

Two whole days and my head is still spinning from Naples. Is it possible to be in a life-induced hangover? Jay has been hovering near me. Swooping in and swooping out to ask me: how am I feeling, and what can he bring me? Do I want to go to the pool or to the spa? Would I like to do the tunnels again? He avoids any direct reference to clowns or acrobats or whatever they were.

I don't really remember the ride back to the hotel, but I do remember stepping into our room, wrapping my clothes in a laundry bag and saying to Jay, "Burn them, throw them away, nuke them. Do what you want with them, but I never want to see those things ever again." I stepped into the shower and stayed there for an hour, detoxing, scrubbing and exfoliating away all the germs and bacteria that could be lurking in a minivan. On the upside, I have once again managed to evade one of the major *Death by* scenarios that star in my *Death by* repertoire. This trip has been groundbreaking from that perspective – who would have ever thought that I could survive any form of mass transportation? But, then again, I suppose that when one must confront the coming of the clowns and a minivan filled with Chinese tourists dressed like the Napoli regional soccer team, the choice is pretty obvious. Soon we shall leave this hotel and head out to the Amalfi coast. I need to work much harder to stabilize the swinging of the pendulum in preparation for the next conquest: Vesuvius. It is hard to put it out of my mind. The hotel restaurant is decorated with a wall painting documenting the volcano and its eruption. One can avoid the inside of the dining room by sitting outside on the massive deck overlooking the sea, but if you do this, you are effectively sitting with the real mountain in full view. I sit with my back to the mountain, trying not to imagine the churning of volcanic fluids and the movement of the Earth's plates below the surface. My own insides churn and twist with nervous anticipation. I increase my attempts to meditate, alternating between sitting and standing positions. I find myself unable to concentrate, unable to block out the noise. My inner voice tries to direct my inner self to remain absolutely calm.

You are calm and quiet and sailing to a happy place, my inner voice instructs.

Liar! I answer back to myself.

You are shaking out all your fears and all of your tension and you feel nothing but peace, my inner voice tries again.

Not true! I respond dismissing myself aggressively.

You are a flower, moving in the breeze. You can feel the gentle tickle of butterfly wings as they flutter past you, my inner voice tries again.

Ridiculous, I am simply and utterly ridiculous! I say and push my inner self's face down in the dirt and rub it in deep.

We are lying on deck chairs in the sun, by the beach. My scarf is hanging from the massive canopy, an extra layer of shade. I am sharing my frustration at my failed meditation attempts with Jay. I demonstrate how I do it, scrunching up my body tensely from face to foot and then releasing abruptly. Scrunch and release, scrunch and release. My muscles ache from the effort. "You see," I tell him, "I do this and then I work on guided imagery. Scrunch and release. *I am a ray of the sun.* Scrunch and release. I *release my light upon the land.* Scrunch and release. *My light is warm and pleasant.* Scrunch and release. *My light is warm and soft.* Scrunch and release." I demonstrate the muscle tension and then the relaxation. "I cannot understand it," I tell him, "I fail every single time. I cannot become the sun ray. All that I am feeling is acute muscle spasms. I think I need a muscle relaxant, but I don't think I brought one. Do you think that garlic will help?"

Jay looks at me thoughtfully and then tells me that meditation and yoga can never be done properly when one is angry or worked up. "Dammit, I know that." I tell him, "that is why I am trying to bloody calm down in the first place." Jay raises an eyebrow and gives me a knowing look. "I am not becoming like my mother and if you continue to talk like that, I will scream." Unwittingly I fold my arms into my standard "fetal position." He notices and covers his mouth to hide a grin. I catch myself, unfold my arms hurriedly and yell "Come on already," spring off my deck chair and fly into the sea.

Jay

Emma thrashes through the water, but soon the thrashes become more consistent and less angry. Her arms stroke the blue waters, and she rides the waves like a water nymph or sea goddess. Perhaps, I think to myself, she should try to meditate in water.

Tonight is our last night at the hotel. After dinner, I pack the car with our luggage, except for what we will need overnight and for our day trip to Pompeii and Vesuvius. It takes me half an hour to get things in place. I am not sure why, because we have bought nothing. In fact, we have had to purge a few items of clothing following the day spent in Naples that ended in the minivan getaway. *Perhaps this car is getting smaller?* I think irrationally. I slam the door shut and head back to the hotel. I go to the reception to pay our bill, and Lucia is there as she was on the night of our arrival. When the transaction is complete, I thank her and wish her luck with her studies. She smiles at me shyly and hands me a picture of a bush sculpted in the form of a mermaid. She has been working on it for several months now. It is her final project for landscaping studies.

"It's not finished yet," she tells me, "but when it is done, she will have long flowing hair, and she will be diving into the water."

"Wow, this is really impressive," I say, "what do you call it?"

"I call it the *La Sirena Serena* – the serene mermaid." Lucia answers proudly.

"*La Sir-Emma Serena*, it's just perfect!" I laugh, "Keep in touch, I want to see it when it is done."

Lucia laughs. "Maybe Emma was my muse after all."

La Sir-Emma Serena – the serene Emma, I think to myself as I go back to my hotel room, – *doesn't seem very likely at the moment.*

On the whole, the modern palette is the same as the one used by the artists
of Pompeii…I mean it has not been enriched.
The ancients used earths, ochres, and ivory-black –
you can do anything with that palette.

Pierre-Auguste Renoir

Emma

Only sadists and masochists are capable of doing what we are about to do. I could not sleep last night. I would not sleep last night. I took medication, did failed meditations, counted sheep, did an inventory of the room, washed the bathroom down with ammonia. I counted the electrical sockets and even flipped through the copy of the glossy hotel magazine. Jay slept like a baby. I wanted to wake him up and shake him and rattle him, and say "Why, why, why are you making me do this?" What kind of sick person goes to see mummified remains of humans from hundreds of years ago? People frozen in action, petrified by volcanic ashes: mid-baking, mid-sleeping, mid-arguing with the neighbor about his barking dog, and then this same person promptly goes straight to the source of the problem, the very reason for the devastation and destruction – an active volcano?

I really don't understand it. It's like an aquarium in a sushi restaurant: it's unnecessarily cruel and sadistic. It is like a death wish, or a self-fulfilling prophecy. We argued about it over dinner last night – as usual, Jay ordered for us: asparagus and beet carpaccio for starters, and then homemade pasta with tuna, capers and olive oil, topped off with white wine. I gave Jay my *Death by* list:

Death by crowds

Death by spiders – *where there are ruins there must be spiders – right?*

Death by rusty remains

Death by petrification

Death by falling off Vesuvius

Death by jumping off Vesuvius

Death by being pushed off Vesuvius - *(maybe that is the same as falling off, the difference of course being intent.)*

Death by lava spillage, fumes, and being burned into human crisps

Jay listened intently and patiently, and then he countered with his own list, using his fingers to number each argument: *First*, it's on the itinerary. *Second*, you planned the itinerary. *Third*, it is more likely that we will be hit by a car – *(thanks a lot for that one, I can add it to my Death by list). Fourth*, you can do it. *Fifth*, you want to do it. *Sixth* and *finally*, I want to do it.

After he had finished listing his points, he lowered his hands and took a deep breath. He looked at me and ended with: "and let me reiterate once more: *you* planned the itinerary and it's on the agenda." Quite brilliant actually. I cannot argue with his logic. I reluctantly concede.

I have set the alarm clock for extra early so that I can do an extra-long health regimen, but there really is no need. One only needs to be woken up if one actually gets some sleep. By the time Jay jumps out of bed, I am packed and ready and slightly hazy from lack of sleep, or perhaps from digesting half a bottle of homeopathic stress aid drops. It says to take them whenever you feel the need, but particularly to be taken when under duress. Pity they don't have a family pack or an intravenous drip.

I drag my way through breakfast, ignoring Changming and the group, who greet us with enthusiastic waves. I avoid the glances of all the servers and receptionists and other hotel staff who are generally so happy when I smile in their direction. The German family left yesterday, but I definitely would have ignored them too. I need to gather all my strength in preparation for this day. I am awake enough to send soulful glares in Jay's direction, but he remains oblivious, completely un-empathetic.

"It's weird, you know, I haven't any clean shirts left. I could have sworn I packed more. I am going to need to buy a few, or at least perhaps wash some by hand."

Does he think that the thought of handwashing and cleaning will make me feel better, cheer me up? Well, it doesn't. I ignore the hint and shrug.

"Oh well, never mind," he says downing his espresso in a single shot.

"Eat up, my darling, we have a long day with lots of exercise in the big outdoors; it is going to be amazing." He is in his element. Flexing and stretching in the hotel restaurant, ready to resuscitate petrified cattle at Pompeii through the power of his optimism. Give me a break.

"I'll wait for you outside, my love. I need to stretch my legs before the drive." He plants a kiss on the top of my head and walks out.

I take extra-long to finish my cappuccino and for the first time ever, I go to the buffet and help myself to an almond cookie, a piece of peach tart, and some smoked salmon on a garlic-flavored, salty cracker. I know it is stress eating, but in fairness to me, it is also avoidance. I am thinking of other ways to stall when my phone bleats like a goat. Jay must have been playing with my ring tones again. Whenever did he find the time? He must be calling to see where I am. I answer quickly and irritably, a half-eaten shard of cracker still in my mouth. "I am coming, I am coming, and you have to change my ring tone back. Everyone is looking around to find the bloody livestock in the dining hall."

"Emma," says the voice.

Oh no, I thought. "Hey Mom."

"Emma, I have no idea what you are talking about, what's going on?"

"No nothing, I just thought you were Jay, never mind. What's with you? How are you today?"

"Well, you know it's final: the dog is dead. Gypsy is gone. Jackie is simply devastated."

I took a deep breath and swallowed the remaining piece of cracker. "I am so sorry." The dryness of the cracker made me want to cough. With a broken voice, I continued: "I will send Jackie a message as soon as we are done talking. It is very sad. Poor Gypsy. Poor Jackie." I start to cough.

"If you hadn't gone to Italy, this wouldn't have happened."

"Mom," I say in-between coughs, "Gypsy has been sick for five years now, and he is…was a dog. Their life spans are shorter. Besides which, death is inevitable." The staff are eyeing me nervously. I signal to Carlo to bring me some water. Changming is watching me too. He looks ready to pounce into action. I must restore control.

"I told you, bad things happen when people travel. Last time, you went to Turkey and your father had to pass that kidney stone." Carlo brings the water to me and I drink as Mom continues to talk, "of course death is inevitable, I have been on the verge of death for years now. On the cusp, on the brink, holding on by a thread, and each time I have been spared, who knows why, when I suffer so much."

I hold my hand over the phone for a second. "*Grazie* Carlo." I say, "Thanks so much. I feel better now."

"*Prego*," Carlo beams and walks off.

Mom continues, "but do you hear me complain? Never! I am always cheerful and happy."

"Yes, well thank goodness for that," I say.

"Why would you put yourself in this situation anyway?"

"Mom, it is more likely that I will be hit by a car back at home than that anything freaky or out of the ordinary will happen to me here." *Dammit Jay for getting into my head.* "Don't worry, I am OK."

"I worry. I am a mother. That's my job," she says in a resigned voice.

"And I appreciate that, I do. But everything will be fine. I love you. Everything will be OK."

We speak for a few more minutes until I am sure that she has settled down. Then we hang up. I gather myself together and head out to Jay, quickly sending a message to Jackie along the way.

Heard about Gypsy from Mom. So sorry. Love you.

To which I get an almost instant reply:

Thanks Emmy. I am very sad, but he was so ill, and contrary to what Mom says, it has nothing to do with you. Enjoy Italy. Love to Jay.

Jay

This time it wasn't me. I swear. I am not omnipotent, and I don't have the psychic powers to will Emma's Mom to call, let alone to knock off an innocent dog. But I could tell as soon as I saw her that they had spoken. She marched into the car park like a soldier on a mission, her feet stamping on the dusty concrete and her arms folded tightly beneath her chest. "So how's your Mom today?" I ask her. "Oh, she's her usual chipper self," Emma snaps and slams the front passenger door shut. The parking lot echoes with the sound of the shrill bang; I could have sworn our tiny little car shrunk a little bit more at Emma's rage. "That good, huh?" I ask rhetorically, and ease myself into my regular squat position. "She told me that Gypsy was put down."

"Oh, poor pooch. Poor Jackie – she must be devastated. That is sad news. Are you OK?"

"Yes and no."

"Because of Gypsy?"

"Because of everything: dead dogs, neurotic mothers, mourning sisters, foreign travel, failed meditation, exploding volcanoes…"

I am glad to be conspicuously missing from the list. "Honey, there is nothing here that you can't handle." I say to her emphatically.

"How do you know that?" she asks in a small voice.

"Because, that is who you are. You are strong. You have fears and you face them." I turn the key in the ignition, and the white rental comes alive. Emma says nothing. She sits back in her car seat and shuts her eyes so tight that I can see the lines of tension forming on her face. I leave her be. She needs some time to herself.

Pompeii is nearer than we thought. I tap Emma on the leg as we pull into the modern city called Pompeii. Regular people live here, work here and raise their kids here. A lot of them live off the tourism industry in and around the ancient ruins. Emma's face is frozen in a position of misbelief and distrust. "How can anyone live here?" she asks, "They should change the name of this place from Pompeii to Denial," she suggests. "Just imagine making your home on the volcanic ruins of your ancestors, knowing full well that you can land up in the same place. It is really macabre."

"There are entire cultures that believe that their dead relatives hang around after their demise. In places like Papua New Guinea, they even keep the skulls of the deceased in a place of honor inside the home," I say.

Emma has no response to that. She's probably the one who taught me those facts in the first place. Instead, her response is to shrug and shiver. "It's creepy and it's sick," she whispers. I have been hearing those words a lot in the past few hours. We are in the ruins of Pompeii, and even before you enter the grounds, there are display rooms showing the petrified forms of humans and animals that have been retrieved from the archeological digs. Emma has been walking around, her shoulders stiff and tense, partly because of the "putrefied smell of death and atrophy" and partly because of her general fear of falling or tripping or coming into contact with rusty objects, crowds, insects, and so forth. She is generally not a superstitious person, or so she claims. Truthfully, I only partially believe her. But today, she is not only chewing garlic to ward off infection, she is also fingering it like a rosary in her pocket. (I must be the luckiest man alive, only someone with anosmia could be with Emma while she devours all this garlic.

Yup, I have no sense of smell whatsoever, ever since that concussion from falling off that ostrich in South Africa. It must be fate. I am truly blessed.)

What the garlic chewing does mean is that this time, as Emma makes the rounds of the area and imparts her knowledge about this place, very few people try to join us and listen to her pearls of wisdom. There is an invisible band of garlic that, like a magnetic field, repels any passers-by from wanting to stick around to hear what this tiny woman with the surgical mask and condiment rosary is talking about.

We examine rich colored portraits and frescoes with scenes of feasts, pomp, and sensuality. We walk from building to paved street to the remnants of the funeral shrines, and consider the grand and sophisticated architecture. We look at sculptures of animals and people. We examine bone shards and pottery shards, seeds, plants, grains and wine jars, coins and jewelry, and the tools of day-to-day trade, all captured and frozen in time. From all of this, Emma conjures up a magical reconstruction of the city throughout the ages. She tells of some of its inhabitants – regular people like bakers, merchants, and blacksmiths, as well as wealthy and privileged Romans who came to vacation on these fertile grounds in order to partake of sumptuous feasts, get drunk from local wines, dine on fruits and nuts, eat the locally baked breads and pastries, enjoy the swimming pool and public baths and not least of all, to attend cultural events at the amphitheater. Come to think about it, it's a little bit like what Emma and I are doing in Italy ourselves.

When Emma is done talking, she is exhausted. We sit on the floor of the Forum on Emma's scarf. The Forum was once probably a thriving and busy marketplace. We imagine ourselves to be like tiny grains of sand in the history of time, not even a speck on the radar of the history of the universe. Behind us, just about thirty kilometers away, Vesuvius looms above and winks in the sunlight.

The fear of death follows from the fear of life.
A man who lives fully is prepared to die at any time.

Mark Twain

Emma

There are twenty-six-and-a-half kilometers between us and Mount Vesuvius. It is thirty-nine minutes away by car. About two thousand years have passed since the famous eruption that destroyed Pompeii and resulted in these ruins. It has been over seventy years since Vesuvius last purged itself in an eruption of significant severity. Since the original fatal eruption, there have been hundreds of minor earthquakes that have shaken and rattled the land. Three million people live around these parts, six hundred thousand of whom have homes in the direct and immediate impact zone. The ruins of Pompeii welcome about two and a half million tourists each year. On the way back to the car, Jay bought a *Pink Floyd Live at Pompeii* T-shirt.

I cannot see Vesuvius, but I can feel its formidable shadow coming for me.

When Vesuvius erupts, it doesn't just release lava; it shoots and explodes lava. You cannot run. You cannot hide. It is an angry and passionate beast. It is estimated that the eruption that destroyed Pompeii erupted with the force of a hundred thousand atomic bombs, exploding tens of kilometers into the air. Jay stops to get a gelato. Something sweet for the road.

"Do you prefer pistachio, or something with mascarpone?" I look at him blankly. "Oh never mind," he says beaming, "I will surprise you."

I keep my eyes tightly shut so that the shadow will not blind me.

The height of the volcano is a pittance – barely one thousand three hundred meters tall. The slopes are marked with both the scars of lava flow and lush vegetation. Four hundred thousand visitors have been brave enough – or stupid enough – to climb that ticking time bomb.

I cover my mouth and nose with an extra surgical mask. I don't want to inhale or swallow the shadow.

"Look Emma, mine came with a wafer. Want to try some? In the end I got you something with chocolate. It is as delicious as it looks. I know because I tried it. I couldn't resist it." Jay laughs at himself.

I pull my scarf tightly around me. I don't want the shadow to touch my bare skin.

Beneath the volcano, two tectonic plates meet: the African and the Eurasian. Even below the surface, there is a clash of cultures.

The shadow sounds like scraping metal and it smells like burning rubber.

We are in the little rental car now, making our way to the meeting point where we will catch a shuttle that will drop us at the base of the mountain where we will begin to climb. Jay is singing, imitating Dolly Parton and Kenny Rogers singing "Islands in the Stream." He alternates between his falsetto and his regular voice.

My voice has gone off somewhere to hide from the shadow. I cannot summon it, no matter how hard I try.

The volcano has erupted at least thirty times since Pompeii was destroyed, maybe more. On at least one occasion, Vesuvian ash travelled as far as one thousand two hundred kilometers away, raining onto the historic city of Constantinople, better known today as Istanbul, all the way in far off Turkey.

As we get closer and closer, I feel like I am being swallowed up by the shadow.

We are at the meeting point, waiting for the shuttle bus. I am sitting in the car. I am doing breathing exercises without breathing and attempting meditation with the shadow knocking on my shoulder waiting to be let in.
Inhale, Exhale.

I choke on some shadow and spit it out straight away.

I am a cloud. I am floating in the sky.
I am a cloud. I am made of ash and vapors and volcanic dust.
I am a cloud; I am floating in the sky.
The sky is red, red, red and so very hot.
"Ems, my love, the bus is here, let's go," Jay says appearing suddenly like a ghostly apparition in the car window.
I grapple with the shadow. But it is a losing battle. My body makes a desperate attempt to stay where it is, but the shadow pushes me forward.

Vesuvius wants me. Vesuvius needs me.

As the shadow propels me forward, I manage to reach into my travel bag with all the provisions. I want to grab my pump and inhale it all in, but I can't. I want to swallow some anti-stress syrup and down it in a few gulps, but I can't. The shadow is bigger than me and stronger than me. So I grab the biggest and bulkiest item – the last weapon that I have against the shadow – the Gulf War era gas mask. "OK, then, let's go." I shout at the shadow – a weary and lonely battle cry.

Jay

Emma has been quiet and reflective since our trip to Pompeii. She really takes the story and history to heart. She is so sensitive that I swear I can feel the pain and anguish on her face as she describes the fatal day that Pompeii was buried in volcanic ash and frozen by a heat so great that they really never stood a chance. I know that up until now she has been reluctant to travel these parts out of fear, but she has been absolutely quiet, calm and composed. As for me, this day is only getting better – a shuttle bus-ride to the base of the mountain summit, and from there a brief hike to the top of the crater and all of this in the great outdoors.

We are waiting for the shuttle bus from the designated meeting spot in National Park Vesuvius, along with several tourists of all ages and nationalities. It is already a few minutes late, so there is some chatter, and comments about the "usual lack of Italian punctuality." On the other hand, there is a group of young people, maybe friends, maybe students, who are enjoying the extra time to rile each other up and cheer. "Today, my friends, today we will make a human sacrifice to the volcano god, and it will be...... drum roll... more drum rolls please..." yells a young man with *Keep Calm and Smoke Weed* T-shirt. The others make the *drrrrrrr* sound of the drum sticks. "Debby! Debby!"

The girl named Debby squeals and yelps "Trevor, don't be silly."

"Not Debby, man," yells another a young man with a curly afro. "It has to be a virgin, man." Everyone laughs, except for Debby, who says "ha, ha, ha" and pulls a face.

"Then I guess it will have to be you, Matt," the charming Trevor says to Fro boy." Yeah, very funny, very funny..." Matthew says, "Not true and you know it."

"What's a virgin, Dad?" asks a little girl wearing pink, shiny hiking boots. She looks at Debby with a concentrated stare, probably wondering whether it is like that medal that she got at her dance recital. Perhaps Debby has to try harder to become a virgin.

"Ask your mom, Lexie," says her father.

"Michael," says her mom indignantly.

"What Lynne? You're the mother," says Michael.

"I'll tell you later sweetheart," says Mom, "the bus is about to arrive."

As Lexie, the little girl with the pink, shiny hiking boots moans at the injustice of her parents and as the rowdy group of friends bicker and tease one another endlessly, the bus finally pulls up. It is a small Fiat bus, painted in camouflage colors with a caricature of a smoking Vesuvius at the side. This will be our chariot to the base.

I run up to the car and call Emma from the car window, "Ems, my love, the bus is here, let's go." Emma is sitting in the car with the doors tightly shut. She turns to me, a little startled. I give a wave and turn away. "OK, then, let's go," she cries.

"I'll save you a seat," I yell back at her and I take my place in the quickly forming line.

Emma is the last to get on the bus. Everyone is seated and ready to go. Just when I begin to wonder what is taking her so long, I hear a bit of commotion coming from the front of the bus. Maybe she needs some help and encouragement, I think to myself. I have been a bit hard on her. This hasn't been an easy trip. I slip out of my seat and in two easy strides, I make it to the driver. He is standing on the steps of the bus and shaking his head at Emma:

"*No signora, non è possibile salire sull'autobus indossando quella cosa. Assolutamente no!* – No, you cannot get on this bus wearing that thing. Absolutely not!"

Emma is standing in front of the bus wearing a gas mask on her head.

Emma

The shadow is all around me. But it can't get inside of me. I am protected by the mask. I am ready for lava rain. I am ready for a molten melt down. I have quite an audience, but I don't care. Vesuvius wants me. I am ready to be engulfed by the shadow in the crater of a volcano. I have come prepared.

The passengers on the right side of the bus are staring at me. Maybe they are staring at the shadow. Some are aghast, others are laughing and pointing. The driver's opinion is clear: he is not letting me get onto the bus at any cost. The only thing I can understand from what he is saying is "no *signora*," and the rest is Italian gibberish. He is blocking the entrance to the bus as if he were a bouncer in an exclusive club and I was some sort of sorry excuse for a human being. He of all people must know that Vesuvius will not be denied. Can't he see that the shadow has me in its black claws? Jay steps in front of the driver, giving him a gentle shove to the side. "Give us a minute, *uno minuto, per favore.*" Jay says to the driver.

"*Che pazza. Cosa sta facendo? Siamo sotto un attacco biologico?* – Crazy lady, are we under some kind of biological attack?"

The driver shrugs his shoulders up and down and continues to mutter to himself in inaudible Italian.

"Ems, Emma, my love, what's going on?" Jay asks. He reaches out for me. I flinch. I can't let him touch me, or else the shadow may come for him too.

Jay

She won't let me touch her. She won't let me come near her. Who is this person? What is wrong with her? Emma is in front of me, but she is all wrong. Forget the mountain. Forget Italy. Where is my wife? How did this happen? When did this happen? How could *I* let it happen?

"Emma," I say, "Emma, it's me. It's only me. You are OK. Everything will be OK." She takes another sharp step back. "No," she shouts "the shadow!"

I look around to see what she is talking about but all I can see is a dusty mountain path and hundreds of trees.

"Emma," I say, reaching out to her, "there is no shadow.

There is no shadow. It is just me." I take another step towards her. "It is just me. Emma. *Look at me.* It is just me."

"No!" she cries.

"It's me. Emma. It's me," I implore.

She looks up at me slowly, and then, with sudden recognition. "Jay," she says, "Jay!"

"Yes," I say, "It's me. Emma, it's me."

"I am sorry," she says, and collapses with a sob in a heap on the mountain path.

Emma

The shadow is gone. The black claws have receded, melted, dissipated. I am on the ground, unraveled and broken. I cannot hold in the calm. I cannot keep the composure. I am done, finished, shattered and destroyed. I am a broken vessel made of shards of mud and tears. I can feel Jay bending over me stroking me, calling my name. But is too late. This place is the end of me. My mother was right. I can't do this anymore. I can't be strong. The volcano should erupt right now, and cover me like a blanket so that I can stop crying and sleep.

"Emma," says Jay. "Emma, it's me." *I know it's you*, I think to myself, *I can see you now. But I am not me. Not anymore. I just want to sleep.* The world has lost its center. Everything is off. We may be alive, but we are no better off than the frozen civilization of Pompeii. For how long can one live in fear? For how long? "Emma, I love you," says Jay. "You can do this. I am here."

"I can't do it, Jay. I just can't." I sob. "All those people dead, all the danger and the risks that I just can't mitigate. This is just too much. The pendulum has swung too far. There is no longer any balance. I need balance. I need stability." He looks at me, confused. "Emma, I'm sorry, I just can't understand you," he says, "your voice is muffled."

He helps me to unstrap the mask. I take it off my face, but I keep it on top of my forehead. We are both on our knees on the gravelly path.

"I just can't do it," I say, "I can't go up there. I am scared and I am broken."

"I know you are scared," says Jay. "And we are all a little broken. Every single one of us."

"You are not broken. Not like me. I am scared of everything. What if there is an eruption? What if we are covered with sprays of lava and suffocated by poisonous gases? What if I fall in? What if I jump in? What if the shadow gets me?"

"What if, what if?" counters Jay, "What if you don't go up there? What if you don't try? What if you don't get to the top?" He grabs both of my hands, "what if you don't see Pompeii from the viewpoint of the summit?" My eyes are filled with tears. Jay grips both of my hands tightly. "If you don't go up there," says Jay, "then your head will be stuck in those ruins, stuck in the sad stories of lives ended in a flash of an instant. You will be stuck in the retelling of history from the dusty remains, and not from the place of the victor, the winner – the one who understands the nature of the mountain and decides to conquer it!" My sobbing has stopped, but tears are still running down my cheeks. "Emma, you cannot go through life wrapped up like a fragile piece of glass."

I blink away the tears and nod. *Look at me*, I think, *I am a hot, sorry mess!* "Emma," continues Jay, "you can do this. And you don't need this thing!" he says and removes the gas mask. He holds me in his arms and I begin to feel whole again. I melt into his embrace.

After a few seconds, he holds me at arm's length and says, "Where did you get that gas mask from anyway? Never mind that, how did you ever manage to get it into the case?" I sniff and stifle a laugh at the same time, "You know those shirts that you are missing? Well, I guess I did remove a few of them. I'm sorry about that."

"Don't be sorry" he says, "let's just get up." We pull each other up. Jay throws the mask into a nearby bin. It hits the bottom with a resounding metallic clink. He gives me a big hug, "are you ready to get on the bus now?" he asks. I nod and sigh, but don't say anything. He squeezes my hand. We board the bus together. The driver looks at me suspiciously, still shaking his head, but he moves aside to let me board. Some people look at us scornfully, others look away delicately. A boy with an Afro hairdo sitting among a small group of young men and women yells out, "Cool mask, why did you throw it out?"

"Virgin," yells one of the girls at him.

"Mom," says the little girl, "you said you'd tell me later, and now is later. What's a virgin?"

The tension in the bus has broken, and Jay and I take our seats. Am I really the crazy one here? Am I really the one who doesn't get the bigger picture? If I am not fragile like glass, then why do I feel so breakable and weak?

Jay

The shuttle bus bounces us up the mountainside. I barely managed to get Emma into the bus, and now she sits beside me, her face green with nausea. Who knew that the one medication that she didn't prepare was seasickness tablets for nearly vertical land travel? I plead to the powers that be that we make it to the summit without further incident. I can feel the driver's eyes on us every minute of the climb. Pine trees bounce in and out of sight. Dense foliage of all sorts wraps and curls around either side of the road for some of the way, and an open drop lay in wait down the slope. The road, at times, is narrow. Very narrow. "Emma," I say happily without a second thought, "open your eyes, look how narrow it is. This is great preparation for our drive to the coast".

Emma keeps her eyes tightly shut. She squeezes my hand till it almost hurts. Whenever the shuttle turns a corner, the driver slows down just a bit and honks his horn, a warning sound just in case there is another shuttle driver doing the descent, who would like to enter the narrow road at the same time. The student friends catch on very quickly and each time the bus turns, they begin honking and beeping of their own accord. Debby, not one to honk or beep like her friends, simply yells out, "We're falling, we're going to die, goodbye Mommy, goodbye Daddy."

The friends follow her lead and start yelling their last and final messages:

"I don't want to die."

"Tell my dog I love her."

"Sorry, I burned down the kitchen."

As the shuttle zips merrily around the corner, they all lean sharply to the left or to the right, depending on the direction of the curve.

"Are we going to die?" asks little Lexie. "Mom, are we going to die?"

"Of course we aren't Lexie, my love," she answers firmly, "they're just kidding around." She turns around and gives the group the stare of death in an attempt to shut them up, or at least to get them to change their tune. Emma is not the only one willing the shuttle trip to end.

Emma has her eyes closed shut. She is counting. The counting is irregular: *seven*, silence, then more silence. *Eight, nine*, silence, then more silence, and then even more silence. *Ten, eleven, twelve, thirteen*, then silence. There is a kind of rhythm to her counting, and I soon catch on. She is counting the bumps in the road. A hundred and twenty-three bumps later, we arrive at the base. From here we will climb the rest of the way to the top of Mount Vesuvius and walk our way around the crater of the volcano.

Emma

Everything that we have done so far has been leading up to this very moment. I feel sick inside. Not only because I am still shaken and weary from my meltdown. Not just because the shuttle ride shook and rattled me, and turned the juices inside of me into churning waves of bile. I feel sick from an acute sense of disorientation. I feel sick with fear.

There is a certain cognitive dissonance getting off the shuttle bus on a trip that has stimulated several really highly probable *Death by* scenarios, only to find yourself willingly climbing the crater of an active volcano. I guess it is not unlike the feeling of jumping from the frying pan straight into the fire. I feel a definite sense of relief to get off the nauseating shuttle and to be on *terra firma*, along with a suspicion that the *terra* may not be as *firma* as I would like it to be. I am not a superstitious person – not really – but I also don't believe in tempting fate. At the base of the crater, even before we begin the climb, we are met by Luca, our guide. Prompted by me, he reassures the group that all seismic activities are monitored at all times. He explains that it is estimated that based on seismic readings, the regional government can give evacuation warnings as early as up to three weeks before a predicted eruption and that no such warning has currently been issued.

"Let's start climbing," says one of the young men, and he races up the path with his rowdy friends.

"Is that it?" I say to Luca, "that's your assurance to us?" That isn't enough for me.

Luca takes a breath and then continues to explain that the temperatures in and around the volcano are measured at all times, and rising temperatures, which could be indicators of an imminent eruption, are constantly being monitored.

The little girl, Lexie, and her parents set off. As do the South American Bible group and the quiet pensioners who could be from anywhere. I am surprised at their restlessness. But who am I to judge?

Luca himself looks bored, and seems quite surprised that anyone is asking anything at this stage of the climb. But I insist that he continue to elaborate. So he tells us that the gases that are released from the volcano are generally very high in sulphur, and so, the closer an eruption is, one can note the rise in sulphur; therefore, sulphuric levels are also monitored on a regular basis.

Luca's entire explanation could not have been more than a few minutes long, but by the time he is done, no one is standing there but me and Jay. One by one the shuttle passengers have upped and left. I think Luca is pleased with my attention to detail, even if he seems strangely annoyed or inconvenienced. It is true that not all travelers require statistical facts or at least probabilities in order to enable them to calmly begin their ascent, but at the very least, I think it was legitimate for me to validate his competence.

Jay is also itching for the inquisition to end, and I can see him shift from leg to leg, waiting for me to give the green light so we can go ahead. Just to seal the deal, Luca confirms that the current daily readings of seismic movement, temperature, and sulphuric levels are safely out of the range of eruption. As soon as I give Luca the final nod of approval, Jay grabs my hand and runs with me towards the white wooden rail marking the ascending path.

Jay

It was not a long climb, nor was it a hard climb. For Emma and me, who are health conscious and do regular exercise, the path didn't come close to breaking a sweat. I have bigger strides than Emma, and I could have out-climbed her with ease, but the rush was in the crescendo: every step taking us closer to the top. Every jump in altitude, and every glance of Naples got more and more spectacular, the green foliage got greener, and the blue sea got bluer.

There is only one significant reason that I can think of to study the ruins and remnants of the history of mankind and that is to remind us that we are alive.

Emma

It is eight hundred and sixty meters from where the shuttle stops until the top of the crater. The gradient is quite steep at first and then it levels out. I get into a rhythm of walking, breathing and stopping to take in the view. Five steps and stop. One, two, three, four, five… count to five. Five steps and stop…count to five. The view of the bay of Naples unfolds. The crater beckons just ahead. Jay and I walk in silence. He takes two steps for every five and a half of mine; we are in a fully synchronized rhythm. At the top of the crater, different groups congregate in various stages of disarray. Some are being given a historical and geomorphological breakdown of the area and are about to embark on their way around the crater. Others are done walking and are deliberating whether to purchase ice cream, sodas, or souvenirs: magnets with volcanoes, decorative items and jewelry, T-shirts and original volcanic rock from the snack shops located on the edge of the crater. Little Lexie is negotiating with her father. She would like to purchase a rock with the brightest blue crystals.

"Is this original volcanic rock?" the father asks the young sales lady. "No *signor*" she says, "it is a regular rock and the crystal is made in a homemade lab." The father sighs. "So it has nothing to do with the Volcano?"

"No, *niente*," – nothing.

"Great, so essentially I am buying nothing of any value or significance to this place."

"I want it, daddy. Please?!" Lexie implores.

"How much then?" relents her father.

"That will be ten Euros," the saleslady says. "I am just hemorrhaging money on this vacation," the father mutters loud enough for almost everyone to hear. "Thanks Daddy, thanks!" says Lexie. Other groups are sitting at the wooden tables or standing at the flimsy wood rails alongside the perimeter. Video, selfies and panoramic shots are being flashed, set up or retaken. None of this is my concern. Jay knows that from this point on, we will walk it alone. I will tell the story of the mountain and we will marvel at the richly varied and colored rocks and shudder at the vapors and steams that emanate from the crater, a constant reminder that a heart of stone can also melt.

Jay

The crater is not what I had imagined. It reminds me of every soufflé I have ever tried to make: different consistencies of colors and textures, and hollow and dry in the middle. It is hard to imagine that this sleepy rock is a dormant beast.

Emma reminds me to respect and to be in awe of this awkward lump of rock and sand. She points out the tiny reminders and warnings that things are not what they seem to be: the scarred and barren parts of slope where nothing wants to grow, the little machines strategically planted to measure seismic movement and temperature, and of course the tiny shoots of steam, like delicate tendrils that bounce off the rock, eliciting over-exaggerated "Wows" and "Oohs" from the mountain hikers. Emma is unsentimental and unperturbed, now that she has done a complete and thorough risk assessment and understands that her probabilities of *Death by* eruption are miniscule. She walks around cautiously, but confidently.

We are at the end of the trail, and essentially back where we started – at the little mountain kiosk. I buy us two espressos, a bottle of mineral water to share, and two T-shirts; one for me, *Volcanoes are hot* and one for her,

Keep Calm and Climb Vesuvius. "Very funny," she says as I hand it to her.

"Well, you know I didn't pack enough T-shirts and I have completely run out. It wouldn't be very chivalrous of me to get one for myself only." Emma raises an eyebrow and gives a crooked little smile. "Oh well then, thanks!"

Before we down the espresso, I raise my tiny little cup and propose a toast: "To the people of Pompeii whose time was cut short. To Mount Vesuvius – that fickle rock that we have conquered – despite her best efforts to keep us away." I take a deep breath, and continue, "to Gypsy, who led the best life a dog could have." I smile and raise my glass to meet hers. She smiles back at me. We clink our glasses together and sit at the wooden table on the edge of the crater and look out into the spectacular bay.

Emma is the guardian of the clock, the official time keeper. "It's time to go," she says, "we need to make it back in time to catch the shuttle." We gather our stuff and make our way down the mountain path, back to the shuttle. The bay of Naples sinks lower and lower into the horizon as we gallop down the crater.

Forty minutes later we are back in the tiny rental car, leaving the mountain behind us, driving towards the Amalfi coast.

Life is a series of natural and spontaneous changes.
Don't resist them – that only creates sorrow. Let reality be reality. Let
things flow naturally forward in whatever way they like.

Lao Tzu

Emma

We are winding our way along the coastal road. Jay is driving. The little white rental is wheezing and objecting under the strain, but Jay isn't letting up. As he drives, I am on my mobile phone talking to the agent, Deborah, who booked us into our next destination – our holiday villa. I should have known in advance that there would be an issue. Her email instruction was deceptively simple, even quite gracious:

When you are on the road to Sorrrento, give me a call and I will tell you how to proceed. The roads are tricky and GPS will only confuse you. Trust me on this one. I am here to help.

She was right at least about one thing. The roads *are* tricky. They are not only tricky, but they are also treacherous and fraught with hazards. The roads are bordered with walls that look like they are about to collapse, overgrown foliage is suffocating with fruit, and flimsy metal bars separate us from the inevitable death plunge. The odds are really stacked against us given the current driving conditions. I would usually be preoccupied with dying at this point. But I am so angry with the imbecile agent that I have no time or patience to think of the many ways that I might die on this treacherous road. My *Death by* list will just have to wait. I am so furious that I am ready to put my hands through the phone and strangle her with my own bare hands. The conversation begins civilly and quickly deteriorates from there.

...

"We are on the road to Sorrento, can you please give me the address so that I can plug it into the GPS?"

"Well, there isn't an address *per se*. What we are going to do is, I am going to give you instructions to meet our guide, Stefano, and he will take you to the villa."

"That sounds OK, but I would prefer to have the address anyway."

"There isn't really an address, that's why our guide will lead you."

"I don't really understand, but OK, please give me Stefano's address."

"Yes, I am afraid that will be tricky too…"

"Tricky did you say? Tricky…?"

…

I am fundamentally incapable of understanding people who cannot answer simple questions, like *What is the address?*

The main reason that civilization is in decline is because of the weakening of fundamental comprehension skills. Jay has been remarkably calm and composed throughout the debacle. I can tell that inside he is as frustrated as me, but like a rock, he sits strong and moves forward, his knees almost touching his shoulders as he masterfully drives through those tiny streets.

Jay

The roads around the Amalfi coast are sexy: bending and winding and gyrating. You have to have patience. You have to be considerate. You need to wait your turn and then take it when it is your time with determination, agility, and accuracy. You need to know where you are going, even if you don't know exactly how to get there. We were on our way to Atrani. A beautiful dot on the coastal map that we had never heard of before. Emma had been speaking to the agent, Deborah, for a few minutes. The phone was now on speaker mode.

"Tell me when you pass Amalfi, tell me straight away, because if you go past too quickly you will miss the turnoff," said Deborah.

"But where is the turnoff? How do we know if we are in the right place? What is the address?" an exasperated Emma asked.

"Well, that is hard to say," said Deborah, "I guess I could try and explain, but it would be better if Stefano shows you himself once you have reached the meeting point."

"OK, we have discussed meeting Stefano already," said Emma, "and we still need to know how to get to the meeting point. I don't suppose that now you can give me an address?"

"Well," said Deborah, "you drive approximately three kilometers until you get to a really large bougainvillea with dark pink flowers, not white or orange. It is growing next to a really old structure with a fresco of the saints and a little glass shrine. At the shrine, you turn left." This kind of situation is very stressful for the average person. For Emma, it was simply intolerable. With a built-in GPS that came with our tiny rental car, two smart phones with backup navigation and a limitless Internet package, but with no address that could be input, Emma was just raring for an argument. "But give us an address," she said "For goodness sake – coordinates, satellite details, anything. Can you at least *try* to be more specific?"

So Emma persisted and the agent resisted. "Just after Amalfi, on your left you should see a road sign that says Sorrento. Follow that sign and drive and drive until you get to a SPAR supermarket. If you reach the convent, you will know that you have gone too far and you will need to turn around," said Deborah, braving forth. Emma was fuming. She was arguing with every fiber of her being as to why this could not possibly be the way that we get to our destination. But there you have it: Italy is a whole different kettle of fish. I was driving merrily along, following the dips and the curves of the road. Emma and her attempts to reason with the travel agent were like a distant buzz in my ears. I was more or less tuned out and focused on the drive. Bend and wind the road goes: hanging vines with luscious grapes over a rustic roof. Wind and bend the road goes: rows of peaches and apple trees. Twist and turn the road goes: lemon blossoms and jasmine everywhere. Turn and twist the road goes: olive trees. I was entranced by the amazing view juxtaposed with that awesome stretch of the blue coast line. The sea was dotted with big splotches and small splotches of ships that wove nearer and further from the horizon. I was so engaged with the view and the drive and the intoxicating smell of lemon and jasmine, that it took me a few seconds to register the change in Emma's tone. "Heavens above" she said, "we've actually found the supermarket. Jay, you are an absolute miracle worker." I grinned. What a wonderful place, what a beautiful day, what an amazing woman.

The SPAR supermarket was like a hallowed beacon of destiny realized. And as we pulled up tightly against the entrance of the building so as not to block the traffic, I spotted a stocky gentleman, helmet in his hand. He had one foot on his bright orange scooter and the other in the road, as if to defiantly tempt the passing traffic to run over him. He was an Italian caricature from an old movie. Skin brown and leathery. White string vest and too short shorts.

He looked at us and coughed out in a raspy voice from devouring cigarettes for breakfast, lunch and supper, and some in between: "*Ciao, sono* Stefano, *andiamo a casa*, let's go home. Follow me. Keep up. Let's see if you can do it without knocking your pretty little rental car."

We made a U-turn on that narrow road and began to make our way back the way we had come. Just when I thought that we were going to be going all the way back to Amalfi, Stefano suddenly turned off the road and into a hidden gate that led us to an even more narrow path. I held my breath as the tiny car turned into the pathway that led to the villa. It seemed near to impossible that we could make it down the path without scratching or denting the white, shiny rental car.

Emma was wide-eyed and watchful and she too seemed to breathe in, in the hope that her inhalation would somehow trim a few of the edges off of our tiny little car.

Emma

Our holiday villa rental is one of eight small villas carved into the side of the Atrani valley. It is self-contained and even has a little launderette and swimming pool to be used at our leisure. It is at the bottom of the narrowest little path that you can ever imagine. Even the car was wheezing indignantly with effort as Jay drove it slowly to its tiny parking space. This place is overflowing with fruits and flowers and vegetables. It is a veritable paradise overlooking Amalfi, which is just a stone's throw away. A stone's throw, and three hundred and twenty-two stairs. Stefano seems to have some connection to the place – caretaker? owner? It is hard to tell. He didn't apologize for the travel agent's ignorance, but then again, he didn't offer up an actual address for this place either.

I must admit that looks are deceptive, because while Stefano looks a bit like a vagabond biker, he took us around the two and a half room villa, and he was so thorough in his tour that I was completely impressed and engrossed. His tour of the forty square meter grounds took about an hour and a half.

From floor to ceiling, he explained every nook and crevice. He explained how the windows opened, and how to close the cupboard without it creaking. He went over every detail from the microwave, to the toilet, to the key holes, from the air conditioning charges and how they are calculated, to what to do if a stray dog wanders into the area. I briefly wondered whether Gypsy's ghost could make it all the way to Italy. Maybe we should leave the door open, just in case? We did a full inventory of what came with the place – dishes, cutlery, soap, number of toilet rolls, sanitary napkins, four regular towels, pots and pans, tea bags, oils and vinegars and condiments, a deck of cards, etc. When he was satisfied that we understood, he started explaining about the surrounding area: the transportation, buses versus taxis versus our own little car, the history of the place, festivals taking place in six months' time, and exhibitions that ended over a year ago. The wine harvest, lemon harvest, pumpkin harvest, main flora and fauna in the area, religious rituals and processions we should be aware of and hand gestures that we should avoid. Jay mumbled some excuse after the first twenty-seven minutes, and then wandered off, presumably to stretch his legs after the treacherous ride up, but I listened quite riveted. Stefano used a plastic binder to remind him what to talk about and he pointed at the necessary items when the language got a bit too complicated. I asked him if he knew that Vesuvius was actually an active volcano, and he looked at me a bit strangely. I wondered briefly whether I had broken the news to him as well. Perhaps I should have been more sensitive broaching the issue. After an hour and a half, he was about to get into the intricacies of pool etiquette using a comic strip with ducks, when his mobile phone rang and he was called away. He looked as disappointed as me to be heading off. Perhaps it was that darned agent on the phone again. Jay reappeared just as Stefano left. What unfortunate timing. I suggested that we bring Stefano back another day so that he could repeat everything for Jay, but Jay, in that gentle manner of his, said that he trusted me completely to tell him everything that he needs to know in order to manage our stay in this little villa.

So, we are here in our next little home, and apart from the insects, creaking cupboards, possibility of stray dogs, (physical or of the supernatural kind), rich smell of fruits, wind blowing from the valley, shared pool and laundry facilities, and three hundred and twenty-two stairs, it is a perfect slice of heaven.

Jay

I wake up and bounce out of bed. Emma is sleeping soundly. She is so still. She sleeps like a statue. I can't even hear her breathing, but I know better than to check, because the last time I checked her in this position, I panicked and stuck a finger by her nose to feel if any warm air was being exhaled and I inadvertently poked her, causing her nose to bleed. She woke up with me pinching the bridge of her nose, blood pouring out and she was unsettled for the rest of the day. Understandably so. It must have been quite traumatic, even if my intentions were good.

It is six a.m. I figure that I have hours before she wakes up. Yesterday was a travel day and between the long ride, the even longer lecture given by Stefano, the lengthy unpacking session and the mandatory detoxing ritual, I figure that she needs to unwind and recharge for a little bit longer than usual. Even if she does wake up, I figure that she will need to do her morning sports and health regimen. Yes, I am sure she will be OK, even if she wakes up and I am not there. And besides which, yesterday we stayed up pretty late. We got to speaking about our itinerary here in the Amalfi region, and also a bit about our stay in Naples.

Emma, who is usually quite confident, asked me whether I thought it had been insensitive of her to ask Stefano what his planned escape route would be, should he be in the Naples area and Vesuvius would suddenly erupt.

"He gave me such a strange look," she said, "I was just trying to learn from him. Surely this is something that he has thought about? Surely this is something that all the residents here have thought about? What about risk mitigation? Shouldn't there be some app that one can use to calculate the velocity and density of the flow, the severity of the heat, the speed of combustion and distribution of the lava? This app would take all of that information, calculate a safe radius beyond which the lava and fumes cannot reach and all the available traffic routes," Emma rambled on.

"Emma, my darling" I said. "The volcano is active, but the people here simply get on with their lives. They know that if the time comes, they will get the earliest possible notice and do what they can to move out. Hopefully they will also get to go back in again after things have calmed down. They will ride the lava storm until it ends and then simply continue on as best as they know how."

She rolled over from her back to her side and looked at me directly in the eyes. "But how do they live knowing it can happen? Knowing that everything can be destroyed? How are they able to simply not think about the many ways things can go wrong when the risks loom in front of them literally as big as a mountain? I have to sterilize my hands every time I sneeze."

I turned to her and put my hand on her shoulder, "They don't think about it, I guess. They just get on. Sometimes Emma, sometimes, you just have to learn to let go."

"Fuck cautious?" said Emma.

"Yes, my love, fuck cautious."

It's a bit trite, but after that she was on top of me, or maybe I was on top of her, and we both had a lot of volcano waiting to erupt. When Emma lets go, she's way out there. No surgical masks, or garlic chewing or meditation or fear of active volcanoes can hold her back. She's unstoppable.

I was thinking of her biting my ear lobe last night as I was jogging down the three hundred and twenty-two stairs. Yup, I am pretty sure she won't be up for some time now.

Emma

One hundred and seventeen, one hundred and eighteen, one hundred and nineteen; I am unsure how to count these steps. They are like uneven wedges cut into the steep slope of the valley. If there is a wedge that is considerably bigger, surely it should be counted as an extra step? Just like, if you eat a bigger biscuit, you should count more calories. Perhaps I should just choose simplicity over accuracy and calculate accordingly using additional half measures. Jay is waiting for me at the Atrani beach where we will have lunch, but I have no choice but to go back to the villa and begin counting from the beginning.

I retrace my steps, noticing a ginger cat lying in the warm sun on the church steps. Seventeen, seventeen and a half, eighteen… sixty, sixty-one and a half, sixty-three – big step there. There are half steps and steps that are over one and a half. At around two hundred and thirty-one and a half, I notice that there is more than one path that can be taken.

I make a mental note which path I have taken (the route via the fire hydrant, not via the little shrine with a pictures of the saints and the fake plastic flowers) and I continue along down the path. At two hundred and seventy-one and a half, my heart is beating from the many stairs and I am glad it is a cool day, because perspiration is not an option, and my brain is beginning to feel a bit leaky. Around the three hundredth step, I am heavily encouraged when I notice a defibrillation machine wedged into the side of the wall in what is beginning to feel like the end of the steps. Now this is a town that has done proper risk mitigation. I make a mental note of where the machine is, you know, just in case. It took me three hundred and fourteen and a half stairs to get to the ancient gateway at the entrance of Atrani. I must tell Stefano so that he can make the correction in his documentation. I am sure he will be relieved to give his next visitor a more accurate picture.

Jay

In Naples, there are hundreds of shops and museums. There are thousands of tourists who step off trains, buses and taxis, straight into fashion houses and jewelers. In the Amalfi area, there are quaint pedestrian malls and cobbled streets lined with shops and restaurants. But they are a brief distraction – the tourists are mainly here for the water. They lay on the beach on deck chairs or directly on the sandy pebbles, swim, sail or snorkel, or explore the coast by any possible means. The locals are so tanned that they are practically orange. You can tell them from the tourists, because they generally have no tan lines. Another observation – Emma's – not mine: speedos are not out of fashion by any means. I have never seen so many speedos. Emma did a moderate calculation of an average of one hundred and forty-nine men in speedos at any moment in time. This might not sound like much, but the Atrani beach is by no means large. Amalfi is a ten-minute walk away from Atrani; it is bigger and more populated with tourists, shops and attractions, so we reckon that the number of speedos would at least triple.

Emma sticks out like a sore thumb here because she is so covered up. In fact, one of the young muscled men who rent out the deck chairs and beach equipment, with a tattoo of a dragon beginning on his torso and wrapping itself over his shoulder and around his back, came up to her and asked her quite politely to uncover herself so as not to offend the locals. Emma gave him a stare so incredulous and so piercing that the young man started to stutter and apologize profusely for not explaining himself well enough. Actually, he was pretty clear: "Take all clothes off," he said. "Here is for swim, not for *la chiesa* – church. We not like woman on beach with pant and shirt and more."

Under Emma's scornful gaze, he crept away, less swollen and proud than when he arrived. Even the fiery painted dragon etched into his skin looked more subdued. After a few minutes, he came back with another person, this time a young woman, who gently explained again that the beach has certain regulations and etiquette. Emma began to soften up and remove layer after layer, keeping only the hat, the dark shades and a one-piece navy and white swimsuit. She folded her clothes neatly into her oversized beach bag and removed a floral scarf that she draped elegantly over the sun umbrella, resulting in a luxurious-looking cabana tent. Once more, Emma was all covered up.

To be blind is not miserable;
not to be able to bear blindness, that is miserable.

John Milton

Emma

Let's just say that Jay and I are both stepping out just a bit, adjusting to our new surroundings and doing things a bit out of our comfort zone. I have stripped down to my bathing suit and I have found that there are several advantages. Firstly, I genuinely enjoy the feel of the water against my skin. I imagine that I am a fish, well, maybe not a fish, maybe some sort of jellified water creature, and I float under the water surface and one can't even tell which is water and which is me. It's a wonderful out-of-body experience. I glide under the surface and imagine that I am in the heart of the sea, nothing around me but a magical sea world. The second major advantage is that with my giant, floral scarf draped over the umbrella, I have managed to blot out the heavy rays of the sun, one hundred and forty-nine men in speedos, thirteen women who are topless, as well as the smell and vapors of countless cigarettes. I have also managed to avoid misthrown Frisbees, balls and flotation devices, not to mention that I am not affected by the sand, shells and pebbles that are kicked up as people walk by. It's amazing what flexibility can do.

As for Jay, his adjustment is even bolder than my own. This morning, as I failed to meditate yet again under the grapevine by the pool, in between my first inhalation and my second round of aromatherapy, he broke away from today's schedule of beach-lunch-pool, and purchased us tickets to see the Emerald Cave – *Grotta di Smeraldo*. I can just picture him at the ticket counter, enquiring about prices, then stepping away and deliberating. Enquiring about travel times and schedules, and then stepping away and deliberating again. He told me that he walked away from the ticket counter four times before he decided to surprise me. The issue is not so much the caves. As you know, we have already had a subterranean experience and to be honest, I am none the worse for it. The real issue is getting there.

Jay knows my feeling about the cesspool that is public transportation and a sea bus is as public as it gets, even worse than a minivan filled with Chinese tourists. It makes me feel ill to imagine being on the boat with barefoot people clinging to the sides wearing skimpy, wet swimming suits that leave moist puddles on the wooden benches on the deck of the boat. Or, equally heinous is breathing in the smells of cigarettes, beer, spicy chips, gelato and engine fumes all mixing and merging and wafting about. It also sickens me to consider the unpredictable spray of the sea released during the turbulent bumps, which leaves a white, salty residue on my clothes and sunglasses. I don't think I can get on the boat. I don't resent Jay's initiative; I only own the itinerary because Jay doesn't like to plan and I need to plan. But now that he has bought us tickets, he does need to try to convince me to go aboard even at the expense of my physical health and wellbeing. The sea bus is going to depart in about ten minutes and we are still on the platform. He is gently and quietly trying to persuade me. "Emma you can do it. Emma, we are going to see something amazing. There is nothing that can't be washed or sterilized afterwards. You made it through the minivan, and this is so much cleaner."

"How do you reckon that this is cleaner?" I hiss at him.

"Well, for one thing," he whispers back, "it is out in the open, so the germs and bacteria are washed away; they don't sit and multiply. For another, the sea is a natural antiseptic because of all the salt. It will therefore disinfect any residual toxins. You know this better than me. Em, I have been in India on the roof of a bus with a hundred travelers; this is nothing like that."

"That's hardly comforting," she says.

"Well, it is supposed to be. We are here now. Let's do it… Emma," he continues, "you have climbed up an active volcano. Let's just go for it."

He talks to me as if I were a young child, coaxing me as gently as possible, but at the same time promising me the intangible reward of growth, engagement and wisdom. "If you do this, just imagine the beauty you will get to see, just imagine what you can tell your mother, the things that you will be able to describe to others."

I am clothed in my layers again. Jay is carrying my bag over his shoulder and he is guiding me by the elbow with his other arm. He is whispering in a gentle voice and soothing me, leading me closer and closer to the perimeter of the boat. I am working up the courage and we are stepping nearer and nearer to the dreaded vessel. There are others around us, our fellow travelers, who can see that we are working through something, although it is not clear what. "Fine," I said, "OK, but I refuse to touch the sides of the boat. You are just going to have to help me over."

A wave of relief washes over me. The captain, a distinguished-looking gentleman wearing a navy uniform of sorts, a peaked cap and a pouch around his neck in which he stores the tickets, is waiting for the final passengers to board the boat. When he sees us, he hops off the boat and rigs the ropes even tighter so that the boat is even more stable and secure for boarding. We are right near by him and he and Jay exchange looks. He comes up to me and says, "*Signora*, please, I help you." He leads me to the step and calls to his crew:

"*Alessandro, Giovanni, venite qui*" – come here. Two young men, dressed just like him, leap forward.

"*Venite aiutare questa bella signora a salire a bordo della nave. Lei è cieca.*" The one gentleman steps off the boat and picks me up like a sack of feathers, and passes me over the threshold to his colleague and into the boat. They lead me to a prime location at the front of the boat, where I can watch the seafaring traffic: yachts and cruise ships, pedal boats and kite surfers. They uproot three kids in the process, who are not impressed that I have taken the place that they got to first.

"It's not fair," they say. "Mom, do something. Dad... come on, say something. We were here first."

"Shush, don't make a scene. Quiet," say their parents, hoping to maintain a low profile.

"Thank you so much." I say to the parents. "You are so kind."

"Oh, it's nothing, dear," says the mom. "You just enjoy the ride." The kids moan loudly and settle down elsewhere.

"*Grazie mille*," I say to the lovely Alessandro and Giovanni.

"*Per niente, Signora,*" says Alessandro.

"*Prego, prego,*" says Giovanni.

Jay is not far behind me. He too has thanked the captain and given him our tickets. He settles down in the seat next to me, looks at me sheepishly, puts his head really close to mine and begins to whisper in my ear. I stop him. "There is really no need to coax and persuade me anymore," I tell him, "I am here and I am settled, and..." But he interrupts me. "Emma," he whispers, "the captain and crew, well, they think that you are blind."

Jay

The sound of the revving engine and a well-timed surge of a wall of water that breaks onto the dock as the boat pulls out, blocks out Emma's audible gasp.

"What? Blind? How is that even possible?"

"Emma," I say, "I am begging you, please just do it. Please just pretend to be blind."

"No, no, no, it is an affront to blind people everywhere. I can't, I won't."

"Emma," I plead, "The captain is watching, he is watching." Emma is shaking her head.

The captain comes over and puts his hand on Emma's shoulder.

"*Signora, non si senti bene?* You not feel good? You need something?" He says very loudly.

Emma shakes her head more profusely. "No, no *grazie* no, I am fine. Really. Thank you so much."

The captain walks off.

"This is wrong, Jay," she hisses, "it's just wrong."

"I know, I know, but I don't want to disappoint the captain. He has been so kind."

"Disappoint him? I think that he will be thrilled to hear that I am miraculously cured." The captain comes back with a glass of water. "*L'aqua per la signora,*" he bellows and places a glass of water firmly in Emma's hand. He walks off again.

"For goodness sake, I am blind, not deaf," Emma hisses at me again.

"Emma, please, let's get through this cruise. It will be an hour from your life. Please, for me. Please, please." I give her my best puppy dog eyes, which despite her sudden "blindness" seems to do the trick.

"I *will* go blind if I continue to see you like this," she says, "Oh well, OK, fine then. But you *will* go to hell for this."

"I know, I know." I say.

The boat trip wasn't a long trip. But it certainly felt like forever. When we docked at the entrance of the watery cave, Giovanni and Alessandro appeared from nowhere, and helped Emma out of the boat, carrying her part of the way. With every step the threesome made, I could feel myself getting angrier and angrier. They led her slowly and gently into the cave, clearing the path of all obstacles, cushioning her from the low walls and leading her around or over the still, shiny puddles. They minded her every step tenderly and with care. They gave her instructions in low, breathy Italian undertones. They were out of my earshot – I could only imagine the seductive words that they whispered so sweetly to my not-really-blind wife:

'We are getting out the boat – *can we gently stroke your arms?'*

'We are now walking – *you are so beautiful!'*

'We are entering the cave – *a place where lovers come to be alone.'*

'We are now heading towards another boat – *where we will make you happy…'*

'We are stepping into the boat – *gently, bellissima, gently sit right here next to us. Does that feel good?'*

My anger spurs my imagination to run wild. My stomach feels queasy. Maybe I will vomit.

Alessandro and Giovanni lowered her slowly into a rowboat in the cave. They sat her down gently. I watched as Alessandro leaned over her, and took her hand. He led it into the water so that she could get a sense of the distance of the boat from the water. I think I growled. Giovanni whispered something into her ear. She smiled a warm, bright smile. What could he possibly be saying? I wanted nothing more than to knock Giovanni and Alessandro's heads together. I thought to myself, what have I done? What have I done?

As I felt sicker and sicker, Emma seemed to enjoy the ride more and more. I sat right behind her, next to a bickering Russian couple, and in front of a row of three kids. The same kids that Emma had previously uprooted. There was a twelve-year-old boy who kicked the back of my seat incessantly. He had a brother who was around five years old. This restless little five-year-old spent his time spraying the seat of my pants with a plastic water gun, over and over again. The third child, a bored teenage girl of around fourteen, played with her smart phone as we sailed in the darkness of the cave. Their parents, a nervous couple from the UK, did their best to reign them in. "James," they said to the twelve-year-old, "stop tapping your feet."

"Yes moron, stop tapping your feet." said the sister.

"Kerry, stop calling your brother a moron. Simon," they said turning to the little one, "put that away, the gentleman didn't ask to be sprayed and he surely doesn't like sitting in wet pants." That much was true. As for the girl, every time her parents looked in her direction, she shrugged, pulled a face and tightened her earphones even tighter around her ears.

As the boat proceeded through the emerald waters, the two men, Alessandro and Giovanni, whispered sweet nothings in Emma's ear and held her like she was a precious doll, and I sat back and felt like a real idiot.

Emma

I feel bad. I feel terrible. But I have to admit that the boat ride was so thrilling. Those beautiful, precious emerald-colored, clear waters, Alessandro and Giovanni holding me and whispering the gentle narrative of the cave and its history in my ears. Probably a good thing they were holding me back; otherwise, I might have leaped into the water and just stayed there diving and soaring among the broken statues, alongside the darting fish.

On the sea bus back to Amalfi, Jay was very quiet. We sat next to each other, not talking, taking in the scenic coastline and inhaling the wonderful smell of sea. As we disembarked from the boat, I gave the captain, Alessandro and Giovanni a big hug. Before they could even offer to carry me off the boat, Jay picked me up and whisked me off, not putting me down till the boat was completely out of sight.

"Jay, put me down. Jay, now. Jay, put me down." I started giggling as he bounced me in his arms. Soon giggling turned to laughter. He put me down on a boulder by the sea. I sat perched in front of him, with the illustrious backdrop of the big, wide sea stretching endlessly to the horizon. He looked at me and took off my sunglasses. "That's better," he said and he came in for a deep, long-lasting kiss.

Jay

In the aftermath of the sea bus and the Emerald Cave, we spent a lovely evening in the center of Amalfi. There is no such thing as a secluded spot in this bustling seaside resort. But once we got back to Emma's itinerary, we were able to find a little restaurant with a corner table and candles. I ordered an array of antipasti for starters, grilled swordfish fresh from the sea for our main meal, and peach sorbet for dessert.

All the way to the restaurant Emma was floating on air. She didn't stop to count the tourists walking around barefoot, nor did she comment on the locals shouting out trying to sell their wares. She didn't notice the birds that swooped down to the tables of the different coffee houses and restaurants to steal away the leftover crumbs. She barely even registered the little shop for tourists right on the main street, selling all forms of decorated lemons, paintings, sculptures: some realistic, some abstract, some in papier-mâché, some in clay, and even some made of glass. Glass fruit, an abomination under normal circumstances, would have been cause to head straight home and to hide under the covers after a few rounds of inhalation, with the air purifier working overtime. But this was a different Emma: she hadn't worn her surgical mask for hours, and her hat and her sunglasses were safely in her oversized handbag that I was still carrying. This Emma could not be defeated by the frivolousness of the glass lemons.

To end the evening, the waiter served us Limoncello. "It is home-made," he said. "It is made by my family for hundreds of years with the lemons that we grow." This was our first taste of the locally-made liqueur and it certainly hit the spot. The lemony acidic taste packs quite a punch. "I would like to propose a toast," said my elegant Emma, raising her tiny little shot glass. She stood dramatically: "To the lemon: bright, beautiful and yellow like the sun. It radiates a sweet, welcoming scent from afar, but its fruit is acidic, tart and hard to swallow." My glass is raised. Emma continues: "To people like us who understand lemons – who have the stamina to bear them, and the spirit to appreciate them. To people like us, who know that as lemons burn, so do they cleanse and heal and restore the body."

"To the lemon!" I say as I charge my glass. "And to people like us!"

We were more than a little drunk, but very happy as we headed back to Atrani, and then up the three hundred and fourteen and a half stairs to our little villa.

What we achieve inwardly will change outer reality.

Plutarch

Emma

I can't believe that we have been in this place for three days. I have tried to make an accurate account of what we have done. At times I have estimated but I think that the margin of error is quite reasonable. I reckon that we have walked the stairs, at least eleven and a half times; that is seven thousand two hundred and thirty-three steps between the two of us. Jay is the wildcard here, because yesterday morning, he went out to buy pastries for breakfast, and on his way back, he dropped them in the street, so he went back to the center to buy more.

On his way back to the villa, I called him to remind him to buy some milk, so he headed back to the center again, bought the milk and then made his way home. He is unsure or unwilling to estimate the number of stairs covered in his little diversion. Either way, I reckon that between us, we have completed at least half a marathon. We have swum in the beach nine times, in Amalfi, Atrani, and even in the glamorous Positano.

In addition to Amalfi, Atrani and Positano, we have stopped in Ravello and the port of Salerno. We have driven in the car and sailed on a sea bus. We have eaten six meals in four different restaurants. We have bought pastries on eight different occasions and gelato in six. We have drunk one and a half liters of espresso and one and a half bottles of Limoncello. Jay has dipped in the shady pool of the villa beneath the heavy grape vines every evening at least once. We have come across hundreds of locals and even more tourists and travelers and people who have somehow landed up in this part of the world for no real reason at all, but have nowhere else to be and no reason to leave. We have had sex a total of five times.

We have done two loads of washing. In addition to all that, I reckon that I have attempted and failed at meditation seventeen times. I have berated myself for failing to meditate umpteen times. I have invented fourteen new *Death by* scenarios. I have spoken to my mom twice and berated myself for being angry at her twice. I have wished a thousand times that I could give myself a break and stop being so damn self-critical.

Right now, when Jay and I are together here in Italy, I feel that we have achieved a balance of sorts. But, without Jay, when I am alone in the bedroom, or outside, meditating by myself – when I consider *just myself* – I feel depleted and off center. I have visions of myself lying in a crying heap, on the mountain path near Vesuvius, and I feel like there is a long way to go before my inner equilibrium can be restored. I guess that means that the pendulums are still swinging.

Today, we got up bright and early and went to the port of Sorrento where we paid for a captain of a small boat to take us on a day trip to the beautiful island of Capri. This is not a sea bus, but rather something more upscale. Jay insists. While we are waiting for our skipper to show. I ponder yet again why meditation does not come to me with ease. I explain to Jay how I try so hard to get myself to succeed. I set the scene as optimally as possible. I work hard on finding the right imagery to guide me, and the best possible spot to park myself. I block out everything around me swiftly and without mercy, like a total eclipse of the sun. My head needs to be in a hermetically sealed vault in order to get this thing right. My attempts to meditate are orchestrated and choreographed with intensity and control. With the number of books that I have read, seminars and workshops attended, and considering the thousands of clips that I have watched showing how the masters with the long beards and funny robes meditate, meditation should, at this point, be oozing out of my very pores. I ponder all these things and then say: "Today, I will try to meditate again."

"You will get it, my love," Jay says thoughtfully, "I know you will. Let go of your frustration and you will get it."

Jay

A few years back, I was travelling alone in India and I came across an open market with thousands of stalls and so many more people that I cannot even begin to estimate the number. I also do not have the capacity to adequately describe the sights, the colors, the conflicting smells. I am unable to put into words the movement and motion of the waves of people thronging through the market so quickly and so determinedly, making their way to absolutely nowhere for absolutely nothing. I have been in strange places and done wild things in my life and the adventure thrills me and stimulates me, but that market in India profoundly and deeply disturbed me.

In the clearing between a spice stand, with all hues of colors and smells so rich and so deep that I could hardly breathe, and a rickety table selling shawls and other textiles, sat a traditional snake charmer on a rugged mat on the dusty street. In front of him, in a ratty straw basket, was his partner, a coiled cobra, mostly covered by a dirty, old cloth.

Seeing me step up, the charmer removed the cloth and began to pipe up a tune on his well-handled pungi. A repetitive pattern of notes hit my consciousness like shards of breaking glass on a polished cement floor. The snake rose to its full height, eye to eye with the noisemaking pungi. It hissed and extended its hood. I shivered with fear. As the charmer moved the pungi music-maker, the snake adjusted its position to remain combative and strong in the eyes of its enemy. Half a head from the pungi and the defensive snake, the charmer himself stayed out from reach, but he kept his eye on the cobra at all times. As the cobra moved, he adjusted himself. As it tensed up, so did the charmer. As the eerie dance ensued, I could not bring myself to look away. An uneasy feeling came over me. At the heart of my discomfort, it suddenly occurred to me with horror, that the snake was handling the man, more than the man was handling the snake. I threw a few coins on the dusty street and, I am ashamed to say, simply fled.

I think about that now as Emma explains to me her grievances at her failed meditation attempts, despite her better efforts to manage and configure the situation. I want to tell her that she cannot control it, and that she must stop letting it control her. But this time I know that she needs to figure this out on her own. So instead of sharing my story, I put my hand on her hand and say as soothingly as I can muster: "You will get it, my love, I know you will. Let go of your frustration and you will get it."

Emma

Our captain is approaching. He has a navy bucket hat with a detachable neck flap and shiny sunglasses in which you can see yourself. He is not quite the upscale captain that I was expecting. For one thing, he is young, very young. For another, he rolls cigarettes as he steers the boat towards us with his feet. I would imagine that this impresses some people, but not me. It certainly doesn't inspire confidence. He docks the boat as we wait patiently on the jetty.

"*Ciao a tutti,*" he says. "I am captain. I am Flavio. We are going to have a great day. *Fantastico.* Welcome to my boat. *Benvenuti.*"

The trip is semi-private. We are with a group of four Australians who are older than us, probably in their late fifties, and who are very far away from home. It is early morning but they are well armed with a cooler bag of beers and unabashed light intoxication. Within minutes, without having introduced themselves officially to anyone, we learn that they are Bob and Kayla, and Judy and Dean from Sidney.

"Hey captain, like your ship. But I have seen bigger," shouts Bob to no one in particular.

"Bob, you perv," says Kayla.

"Ka, Ka, Ka Kayla, sometimes a boat is just a boat," croons Bob.

"I know you, Bob, that's not what you meant," Kayla replies.

"Yeah, Bob, you sick old man, we all know you," says the other woman.

"Oh Judy, you would know a big boat when you see one, right?" says Judy's husband, nudging her with his elbow.

"That's for sure," Judy giggles back at him.

"Dean man, whose side are you on anyway?" asks Bob.

"On the side of whoever has the beers!" says Bob. The Australians give a rowdy cheer. I try not to be judgmental, but I can't help rolling my eyes at Jay.

While the Australians make their noisy entrance, two additional travelers board the boat. They are two young French women, both in their early twenties. Flavio the skipper eyes them with keen interest. They make a point of openly ignoring him with an overt display of both contempt and disdain. Just ahead of us, a family from the UK board the ship. They consist of two tired-looking parents and three children, two boys and a girl. The children are pretty young.

I hope this won't mar our trip. Young kids can be quite disruptive. The youngest is brandishing a water pistol and he has also taken an interest in the two young ladies from France. He aims his water pistol directly at their skirt-covered bikini bottoms and shoots little sprays of water as they walk a few steps ahead of him. The one young lady turns around and gives him a big glare. The other just lets off a steady stream of French expletives. The parents look quite preoccupied and unhappy. They stop to introduce themselves to the captain, who suavely salutes them, holding two fingers to the rim of his bucket hat. "I am Flavio," he says, "I am the captain."

"Nice to meet you Flabbier, I am James," says the middle son politely. "His name is Flavio, moron," says the girl to her brother. "That's exactly what I said Kerry, *Flabbier*," says James to his sister. The parents give a weak smile and a helpless shrug and shepherd them onto the boat.

"Come on kids, in you get. Kerry, stop calling your brother a moron. Simon, aim at the water, not at the ladies. They didn't agree to be sprayed." The unhappy family take their place in the boat and await further instructions. The mother puts her hands on her forehead as if she is checking herself for a fever and gives a big audible sigh.

She reminds me of my mother and the conversation that we had just minutes before we boarded the boat. I called her to say hello. She picked up after just two rings. "Hi Mom," I said.

"Good that you remember me," she says. "So lucky that you are having a wonderful time in Italy, when your sister's dog is so sick that it gives up and dies. Every time someone travels, something bad happens. My arthritis flairs, a plate breaks, the Internet goes on strike."

"Mom," I say, "I am truly sorry to hear about Jackie's dog. I have already told you that and Jackie and I have even been in touch, but these thing can happen regardless of whether or not I travel."

"You don't know that," she says. "I believe that there is a connection. Are you at least staying healthy? Taking antacids for the food, antihistamines for the dust, and antibiotics for everything else?" It suddenly occurs to me that it has been two days since I have taken any medication whatsoever. I haven't really needed anything or thought about it. I also haven't chewed any garlic to preempt infection. Goodness me, it has also been three whole days without a surgical mask. *Wow*, I think to myself. *What's going on here?*

"Yes, Mom," I answer, "I am OK and staying healthy. And you, are you OK?"

"Well, I am, you know, as to be expected. At my age everything is broken, but who am I to complain? I am always positive and happy. I never let on how much I suffer."

"Mom, is there anything I can bring you from Italy?"

"Just come home safe and happy. That's all a mother wants. Tell that Jay to keep you safe."

"I will Mom. He sends love."

"Love," she snorts. "I will send it on to your sister's dog."

Jay

They must have seen us before we saw them. We were the last to board. Emma stepped on to Flavio's boat with the agility of a gazelle, sat herself down at the built-in table and helped herself to a closed bottle of mineral water. When I got on the boat, they were glaring openly and whispering. I could catch phrases like "stinky liar" and "cheat" from the direction of the kids and "shame on her" and "fraudulent" from the parents. I could tell that Emma had no idea who they were, and even though they were looking directly at her, she didn't seem to even notice that the comments were directed at her. She must have been practicing meditation. I am always amazed by her ability to completely tune out the rest of the world.

I went up to the parents, steeling myself at their disgusted looks. As nonchalantly as possible, I said, "Hey, I remember you from the Emerald Caves! Weren't they wonderful? Didn't you just love it?"

The mother sniffed, muttered something under her breath and looked away.

The father said, "Yes, sure," in an insipid voice. His wife kicked him in the shins.

"Yes," I continued, pretending to be oblivious of the tension between them, "we also enjoyed it, and our stay is just getting better and better, now that Emma is fully recovered from her surgery and she can see again." I breathed in quickly and gave a dramatic sigh. The wife exhaled and visibly softened.

"Poor thing," she said, "I am so glad that she is doing better."

"Yes, so are we. We were concerned that her recovery would take longer." I gave another dramatic sigh, and then a long pause and then said "Oh well, that's life!"

"Indeed it is," said the husband.

I gazed over at Emma and gave a nod in her direction, "Yes, well, we don't like to talk about it, so best not to say anything to Emma, that's my wife. I am Jay, by the way."

"Oh, OK then," said the husband, giving me a man-to-man conspiratorial nod, "I am Keith, and this is my wife, Sherry." Sherry gave a shiny, empathetic smile.

"Well, hello then," I said, "let's all have a lovely day!"

We all look at Emma, who gives a big sigh. Sherry blows her a kiss of encouragement. "Poor lamb, what a brave girl."

My work here is done. I am simply wracked with guilt.

Emma

Within seconds, Jay, that amazing people person, is chatting away with the unhappy family from the UK. I just know that he will find a way to put them at ease. He has that wonderful quality about him. I am sure that by the end of this trip, he will know each one of Flavio's passengers. I am only too relieved not to have to make small talk, especially since I am focusing on my breathing.

Inhale. Exhale. Inhale. Exhale.

I can hear the cawing of a sea gull. Concentrate, concentrate. Hands at side. Eyes closed. I focus on a drop of water that wafts from the sea onto my skin. I wonder if it is salty or sweet? I have an urge to lick it. I try to refocus on its color. Is it an emerald drop or a regular translucent one? Focus, focus. Focus! Why can't I get this meditation right? I shrug and shake out all my muscles. Start again. This time I don't think of a drop of water. Instead I focus on an air molecule. The air molecule is floating into my body. I wonder, does it come in through my nose or my mouth? My mouth is closed. Must be my nose. Could it possibly enter the body through the ears? Is that physiologically possible? What about through some of the other body crevices? Could those welcome air molecules? My mind begins to wander to the nether regions. Wait, wait, wait, don't go there. Focus, focus, concentrate. A drop of water is not working for me, nor are air molecules; how about imagining that I am a blood cell? I am a blood cell drifting around the inner sea. I wonder whether I am a white blood cell or a red one, or a platelet. I think it is better not to be a white blood cell when you are meditating. They have to work too hard. Oh just forget it. This is useless. Yet another failed meditation. I open my eyes and give a breathy, deep sigh. Jay is still with the family from the UK and they are all smiling. The wife waves and blows me a kiss. Jay has worked his magic again. How does he do it?

Jay

I think Flavio has got it all figured out. He has this boat. He spends his days on the water speeding back and forth and meeting people. This thing that he has here; it answers all my needs. I think I could settle down like this, with Emma by my side, sailing from coast to coast and bringing travelers from island to island, beach to beach.

There is ample space in the hull of the boat for twelve passengers, but Flavio has asked for at least five of us to sit on the bow to "balance out the boat." Emma is all about balance, but this is not a very reassuring request and she is scared to be way up front, so we are not there. Instead, the family from the UK is there. The mother, Sherry is gripping the five-year-old, Simon, practically crushing him. The father, Keith, is sitting behind James, the twelve-year-old, and Kerry, the fourteen-year-old, and they are having the time of their lives. James and Kerry are screaming at every turbulent bump and at the sea spray as it showers down on us. They whoop at the speed, and wave at the other boats, ferries and yachts that pass our way. The coastline flashes past: endless, ragged lines of cliffs, sepia and terra cotta colored villages, an *Amalfitana* tapestry stitched seamlessly between sea and sky.

The two other passengers who have opted to sit on the bow are the French girls. Having stripped down to their bikinis, they are now lathering each other with sunscreen. James takes a few minutes off from enjoying the bumps and turbulence to feast his eyes on the girls. "James, you are so gross! Dad, James is being all creepy,"

Kerry tattles. "James, look away," says Keith gruffly and locks his head straight forward, staring at an imaginary point on the horizon so that his daughter will not have any reason to rat him out as well. The other person who takes a deep interest in the girls bronzing under the Italian sun is the cheerful skipper, Flavio.

Flavio has things so figured out that it took him just a few minutes to confirm that the Australians have boating experience that he can leverage.

"You know how to handle her? She not love everybody," he challenges them.

"Course mate, we're from Sidney," Dean and Bob retort, lapping up the bait that Flavio has hooked.

"You show me, yes," he says, and clears his place at the rudder.

Now that he has palmed off the steering to the Australians, along with the decision of how fast and hard to hit the water, he goes to the starboard side to chat with the French girls.

"You need help?" he asks.

"*Non, merci,*" they turn their backs to him quite deliberately and giggle.

"Come, come, I do you both." He says not so delicately.

"Sure you will, you bastard," says Bob the new co-captain from Down Under and laughs.

The alternative co-captain Dean snorts: "What a smooth operator."

Judy elbows Kayla and says loudly from the hull, "Watch out girlies, the Captain's on the prowl..."

"Can you believe this guy?" I say to Emma. "What a player."

"I haven't been listening," she says. "I have been watching our co-captains steer the boat. They really are quite competent."

I can tell without even asking that on Emma's perpetual mental list, she has happily crossed off risk mitigation for replacement of sea captain.

Flavio pulls out a cigarette and a lighter. He continues. "I had French girlfriend; she is famous singer. You know her? Claudine Morel. We lived in Paris." He offers the cigarette to the girls as if it were a bouquet of flowers. The girls ignore him.

"*You* lived in Paris?" says the one young lady, disbelievingly. "Where? What she sing?"

Captain Flavio nonchalantly shrugs and lights up. He puts the lighter back in his pocket and continues, "yes, two years ago, but now she not my girlfriend. We broken. I not have one now. A girlfriend." Flavio says, and puts on a long, sad face. With a dramatic sigh, he takes a long drag of his cigarette.

The other girl makes a big face of being bored and gives her friend, the sceptic, a warning look. Her friend looks back at her and mutters loudly enough: "Marianne, *C'est un menteur.*" Emma smiles. "What did she say?" I ask her. "That one," Emma says pointing to the blue-bikini girl, "thinks that Flavio isn't being completely honest with that one," says Emma, pointing to the pink-bikini girl.

Blue-bikini girl scowls at Flavio. "I have never heard of this Claudine. I work in French television. What does she sing anyway? You imagine her, right?"

"Monique, *arrêttes! Il est mignon*" – lighten up a bit, her friend implores, "he's cute."

"Don't be silly, he's not cute. He's repulsive and a liar. I bet you he's never ever been in France," the pink-bikini girl says to her friend.

"Where did you live in Paris? What is the address?" she demands to know. But Flavio, undeterred, ploughs forth, trying his luck on the pink-bikini girl. "You, you need more cream, you are white like mozzarella. I call you Mozzarella."

The girl giggles, her friend rolls her eyes. Flavio has scored points with the one and lost big time with the other.

"Hey mate, we don't want to cramp your style, but we want to get back to our friends." Captain Bob says to

Flavio. His friend Captain Dean snickers. "You mean you want to get back to your beers," he says.

"Yeah," says Bob, "isn't that what I said?" Bob and Dean throw back their heads in laughter. Emma sighs.

Judy and Kayla laugh from where they are sitting.

"Well come and get the beers then," says Judy and she pretends to throw the cooler bag over the side of the boat.

"Watch out, I am coming, Jude," says Dean.

Flavio smiles at the girls sweetly. "Enjoy, enjoy, we talk more about Paris. I come back later, *ci*, and put more cream on you, Mozzarella."

He reluctantly crosses the starboard and resumes his position, cigarette hanging from mouth, foot on the rudder, eyes intently on the girls tanning in the sun.

Emma

I would love to join the others on the bow. I am absolutely certain that Jay would be thrilled to be there too. He is looking eagerly at the ample space that is left in the front, but I can tell that he is reluctant to leave me. I wish I could go. I have done so many things this vacation to challenge the *status quo*, but this, this would be too much. I can't help it. I instinctively run a quick *Death by* list:

Death by drowning

Death by asphyxiation from over-oxygenation

Death by blunt trauma (slipping in or off the boat)

Death by boats colliding – is that called a boat accident?

"Jay," I say to him, "go, go sit up front, I will stay here and relax. Maybe I'll try to meditate again." (For goodness sake, who am I kidding?)

"Are you sure, my love? Will you be OK on your own? Is it OK? Are you sure?" Jay's face is bright with hope.

"Yes, yes, sure, go. I will be fine."

He is up and over to the port side in seconds and soon he has seated himself on the bow. Stretched out and taking in the sun, the sea and the spray, he looks like he belongs up there.

I breathe in, inhale and exhale. Relax. Just relax.

Inhale and exhale. Relax my limbs and try to float, float away. I am a cloud.

Be a cloud. Feel the cloud. Dammit, I am a cloud.

Flavio has moved into a new position. He is poised with one foot on the steering wheel and the other on the side of the boat so that he has a better view of the bathing Mozzarella. The foul air from his cigarettes wafts its way towards me. I am unable to summon the cloud inside of me and to float away.

Death by cigarette stench

Death by smoke inhalation

Death by foot bacteria

Death by just imagining where those bare feet have been.

The Australians are reliving a past camping trip involving a massive spider, a guitar, and a box of matches during a campfire on a summer vacation. They are laughing, practically rolling around in the hull.

Death by arachnophobia

Death by fire

Death by bad music

Death by other people's memories

Death by nostalgia

"Hey Mozzarella, you want to come here and ride me? *Mozzarella, mi senti? Per favore. Viens ici Formaggina.*"

Is this guy for real?

Death by nausea

Death by bad come-ons and creepy captains

I can't do it, I can't do it, I can't, I can't.

Death by fear

Death by over-thinking

Death by over-analysis

Death by the need to control, control, control

ENOUGH, STOP, ENOUGH already.

I get up – no, I spring up, like an unleashed panther. I jump up onto the port side of the boat and make my way to Jay.

Jay

I am stretched out on the bow. Sherry and Keith and the kids are in a moment of familial bliss and serenity. They are in front of me making happy memories.

Pink-bikini girl and Mozzarella, currently un-harassed by our skipper, are unabashedly tanning, turning over like chickens in a rotisserie to guarantee a consistent all-around tan.

I lie on the deck with my eyes closed. I can feel the sun shining directly onto my lids and the light behind my eyelids feels like the brightest, warmest red.

As I lie there, the light fades from bright red to fuzzy black. I can sense movement and shade. A cloud overhead? Another ship passing by? An ancestral spirit stroking me, causing my spine to prickle? I open my eyes slowly. Emma, like a perfect vision, is standing on the bow, looking over me and out to the deep blue sea. I am shocked and thrilled, and thrilled and shocked. So much so, that I can't think of anything to say. So I just reach out for her and pull her down towards me. She doesn't say anything either. She sits right up close to me and then she stretches out next to me under the warm yellow sun. We lie shoulder to shoulder on the deck of the boat.

*Meditation is the dissolution of thoughts in Eternal awareness
or Pure consciousness without objectification,
knowing without thinking, merging finitude in infinity.*

Voltaire

Emma

I am a cloud. A tiny wisp of a cloud. I am light and effortless.

I am in the blue sky. I am carried like a feather on the currents of the heavens.

The sky is like the sea; it is deep and limitless and has no judgement or reservations.

It accepts me and envelops me like a warm blanket.

I float along the blue sea, until all merges and converges and all that I see is blue.

All that I am is blue.

I am the sea, swirling and whirling and gliding.

I am the sea, breaking on the shores of distant places, breaking over man-made jetties and unspoiled coastline of untouched wildernesses.

I am the sea, entering the nooks and crevices where no one else has ever been, stretching and easing into deltas and tributaries.

I am the sea, lazy and slow.

I am the sea, angry and heavy.

I am the sea, frenetic and agile.

I am the sea, floaty and light, like a cloud moving like a feathery nothing through the sky.

I am a feathery white nothing. I am white.

I am a cloud.

Jay

We arrive at Capri, and the group gets off the boat in high spirits. Flavio has been generous with his explanations of the island vista, steering the boat by low nooks and crannies, pointing out famous houses and landmarks, and making a point of driving through the tunnel of love, where one is supposed to profess one's undying love and to kiss as the boat passes through the narrow and vertical rock formations. The kids call out to their parents "Kiss, kiss, kiss." Keith and Sherry oblige with a modest peck on the cheek. Flavio calls for the two French girls to kiss. Mozzarella laughs and blushes sweetly and the pink-bikini girl lets off a fresh stream of French cuss words.

When we reach the beach where Flavio plans to dock the boat, we patiently wait our turn to disembark. "What are your plans today?" I ask aloud to no one in particular. The Australians tell me that they have lunch reservations in the center of the island, and plan to shop out the place. "We're sure the beach is top class mate, absolutely super," they say to me. "We're from Sidney. We know beaches." The family from the UK are next off. They don't have specific plans, they tell me, but their first priority is to find a public bathroom as soon as possible. "It's urgent, Mom," says Simon. "Right away, we are going to find a toilet right now," she says to him. The five of them hurry off. The French girls show no signs that they have heard the question. I suppose that their plan is to simply transplant themselves from the boat directly onto the beach and to continue rotating like chickens in a rotisserie. Flavio says to the blue-bikini girl as she steps off the boat, "Mozzarella, I come back for you soon, *ci.*" To the other girl, he just glares at her the minute he is sure that Mozzarella cannot see him. If she isn't going to help him, then she is just in the way. We are the last ones off. Emma opens her eyes like a sleeping beauty, as I gently say, "Ems, Emma, we need to get off the boat, we have arrived. Emma, Emma, wake up, we are here, we are in Capri." She looks at me and gives a huge, bright, endless smile. "I did it, Jay, I actually did it. I finally managed to meditate."

Emma

I float off the boat on a cloud of ecstatic joy. I did it. I finally did it.

We are at *Marina Grande* on the beautiful island of Capri. According to our itinerary, we have an agenda that is comprehensive, intense and rigorous. It includes a mini-trek to Villa Jovis, a break for lunch at a local restaurant, which is to be chosen from one of the three options that I have already researched, but that will need to pass my on-site restaurant check. After we have eaten, we will work off the meal with an athletic stroll in the Gardens of Augustus. Finally, we will head back to the beach and have a quick swim, before our skipper, the cigarette-wielding, foot-steering Flavio, comes back to collect us.

That was the plan. But today, I just threw out the book, eliminated the well thought out and heavily researched agenda, and threw caution to the wind. Jay and I rented deck chairs in a secluded, private spot on the big boulders of the Marina, and just lay there, relaxing and chilling.

Occasionally, we got up to dive off the boulders into the brilliant clear waters. Now and then we shared an intimate conversation or just passed a subtle look. We dined out on white wine, bananas and crackers that we purchased at a little hole-in-the-wall store. It was so simple, and so wonderful. Never before has my head been so clear, unfettered and uncluttered. Never before have I felt so calm.

Jay

I swim under the water and imagine a life in this cool sanctuary. There is the life I live at home, the things I have, the work I do, the money I earn. Then there's travel, which gives me the rush of something different, something original, something outside of who I am. Emma swims beside me. We are both under the water, moving forward vigorously and confidently. The current pushes us further out, away from the boulders on which our little corner of paradise is perched. In a sudden rush of energy, Emma charges forward. I push myself with all my strength to reach her. As I surge through the water, my lungs bursting for oxygen, I think that there is no greater rush, no more significant moment, and no more fulfilling venture to be experienced, than to share Emma's success and her complete satisfaction at having reached a place above control and fear, above planning and methodology. A place where she can just *be*.

We float up to the top of the water. Emma makes it to the surface before me. By the time I have breathed my first breath above the water, she is off again, stopping only briefly to make sure that I am following her. When she sees me, she smiles.

It is not lost on me that we are a bit of an odd couple. Her magnetic north is so strongly bound to home, and my spirit is always looking outside and away. While Emma thinks that she seeks to calm the inner turmoil and to find a calm place of being, the way I see it, her real need is to accept the scary, noisy world and not to evade and avoid it. She needs to accept that balance is fleeting, and that equilibrium exists on a gently shifting scale – not on a static, cemented tectonic plate. I, on the other hand, welcome inner turmoil and embrace a dynamic ever-shifting world, at the expense of finding internal stability and harmony.

Contrary to what it may seem, I need Emma as much as she needs me. Emma is my anchor in the imbalance that I seek. We may be swimming in the waters of that beautiful Capri beach, but today, we both feel like we have come home.

Emma

We wait on the dock for Flavio to steer by and collect us. Keith and Sherry, kids in tow, are weighted down with new flotation devices brandishing the Italian flag and peaked caps with Capri written in rainbow-colored shades. They have bottles of olive oil and packs of dried fruits, and a tired little boy, Simon, who is carrying a bucket filled with pebbles and sand that he has gathered from the shores and shallow waters of the beach during the course of the day. They hop onto the boat wearily, but with some relief that the long day is drawing to an end.

The four Australian friends have had a productive day shopping, but apparently an even more productive day drinking. They jump on board together, narrowly avoiding falling over the side. They collapse inside the boat, where they lie blocking the path for the French bikini twins, who are next to climb back into the boat. Unconcerned, the pink-bikini girl steps not at all delicately on one of the Australian men who is sprawled on the bottom of the boat, eliciting a low groan of delight. "That's what I'm talking about, do it again," says the low voice from underneath the bare, tanned foot. The others bellow and wheeze with laughter. Then comes the blue-bikini girl, and in two seconds Flavio steps up to the side of the boat. *"La Principessa, la mia Mozzarella bella.* Let me help you. Here *bellissima*, let me take your hand," and he too trods on the Australian in order to carry his girl over the threshold. This time, the horizontal man is less impressed. "Get off me, you prick," he moans, "or I will snap your leg off like a twig" – there is a brief moment of silence – "once I can fucking move," he finishes off. This time, the bellowing and wheezing laughter from his friends is even stronger than before. Mozzarella swoons and giggles, and extends her white oily hand delicately like the Queen of England. Her friend storms to the front of the boat, muttering under her breath so that everyone can hear her: *"T'es une pute. Je savais que tu choisirais ce connard."* She spreads her towel on the deck and lies down in a huff, with her shirt over her face. Clearly the young woman was quite distraught.

We are the last to board. Jay helps me on, and without hesitation, we slip around the side and find a place on the bow. I am physically on top of the boat, but my heart is still floating in the water.

Jay

The boat is speeding merrily towards the port of Sorrento. Emma is sleeping in the sun, curled up right next to me. She is completely relaxed and calm. In the belly of the boat, I can hear the Australians. They are snoring and snorting; not sleeping, but not completely awake either. The family from the UK are enjoying the sea breeze, and the French girls are tanning. Everyone is where they should be. Only our skipper, Flavio, seems to be pacing restlessly at the rudder. He looks from the horizon to the French girls, and then back again. After fifteen minutes of travel, Flavio is looking for a creative solution to continue to melt his ice princess, the lovely Mozzarella. He calls over to the boys, James and Simon, "Hey, *ragazzi*, you want to be captain? I teach you."

"Mom, can we, can we?" the boys are thrilled.

"Sexist," Kerry says. But she is too busy filming the view with her mobile phone to care.

"Sure. Sounds like fun!" Mom says, and the boys scramble to the hull.

Flavio is a diligent and efficient teacher. He puts little Simon on the rudder and places his hands in the correct position. Flavio says to James, "You help your brother, yes. When I point left," gesticulating left with his thumb, "you make sure he move to left. When I point right," gesticulating right with his thumb, "you make sure he move to right." Flavio demonstrates with exaggerated gestures, "Long point, big move. Short point, small move," staccato thumb movements. "*Allora*, now we try."

After three or four trial rounds, Flavio leaves the five-year-old steering the boat with the help of his big brother. He hops to the front of the boat, half reclining on the bow, and half hanging out over the boat where he can talk to the girls, gesticulate to the boys, and have a clear view of the sea at the same time. While his end game is obvious to me, it still makes me nervous to see the boys in charge and the skipper only half engaged in the action. I will Emma to stay asleep.

"Mozzarella," Flavio purrs, pointing slightly right. "You enjoy your holiday? You like Capri? *Romantico, ci.* You need someone to show you around?" He points a bit more broadly to the right.

Mozzarella's friend interjects. "We don't need a guide."

"Everyone needs a guide. I come to Paris, you be my guide."

"You don't know your way in Paris? You said you lived there for two years. *Menteur*" – Liar!

Flavio points straight ahead with his finger. James looks confused. "Flabbier, what does that mean?" James calls out to Flavio, mimicking Flavio's straight point.

"Straight, this means straight, OK?" Flavio shouts at James. I think to myself that if I ever spontaneously give a passenger the rudder, I will do it only when we are alone on the boat. The anxiety on Keith and Sherry's face is growing.

Mozzarella tries to appease both sides: "No, we don't need a guide, but we want to find a good nightclub."

"Uh, a good nightclub, *buona idea*," say Flavio.

"Flavio," shouts Sherry, "are you sure this is a good idea?" She turns to her husband, "Keith go up there and help the boys."

"No Dad, don't come here, we are fine," says James.

"We're fine…" shouts Simon, "I'm the captain!"

"He says he's fine," Keith repeats loudly to Sherry, as if she can't hear.

"They fine the boys, don't worry. You be proud *Mama*," Flavio says to Sherry, gesticulating broad right and then short left. James adjusts Simon.

After a few seconds of silence, Mozzarella's friend says, "We heard there is a good club in Sorrento."

"Left," Flavio calls and gesticulates. "Clubs in Sorrento are for locals. Lots of fighting. Not good for tourists. *Sinistra*," he yells at James, "more left," and gestures left more broadly.

"No, we wouldn't want to go with locals," says Mozzarella's friend sarcastically.

"More left," Flavio shouts, forgetting to gesticulate.

"There's a ship coming," shouts James.

From where I am sitting, I can see the ship. I am quite sure that it is in Flavio's view. I think that he can see it. I hope that he has seen it. A little seed of panic grows. I touch Emma on the shoulder absently. She is still curled up and asleep. Keith and Sherry are looking increasingly agitated.

"Yes, I see the ship. OK, you are fine." Flavio shouts back to James. "No," he says to the girls, "You need something with more class, *più elegante*. Especially for *la principessa*." Mozzarella giggles.

"A ship, Flabbier," calls James.

"Straight, straight, go straight," yells Flavio to the boys.

"Flavio, you must take over," says Sherry, "We insist. Keith, help me please."

"Right then," says Keith mustering up an authoritative voice, "So Captain, go now and help the boys, then."

I am quite sure that we are not in any danger, but once more I check to make sure that Emma is not awake.

"OK," says Flavio, not sure what all the fuss is about. "I come back," he says to the girls, and springs down to Simon and James.

"OK, *ragazzi*, well done, you are finished, *finito!*" He adjusts the boat's course and puts a hand on each boy's shoulder.

"You be captain like me when you are big?" he asks Simon.

"Oh yes, yes!" says little Simon. The boys start to head back to their parents. Keith takes Simon by the hand only letting go when Simon is sitting securely with Sherry. He then extends his hand to James. But Flavio is not quite done yet.

"OK, you next big man, you be captain without your little brother, *ci,*" Flavio says to James.

James is thrilled, "Yes, Flabbier, thanks!" he calls. "Can I Mom, Dad, *pleeease?*"

Sherry and Keith, so relieved that five-year-old Simon is no longer in charge, quickly relent and agree that James is old enough to manage.

I also begrudgingly admit to myself that I am pleased that someone who is tall enough to actually see the sea has his hands in control of the rudder.

As it turns out, our collective relief is somewhat short-lived. James resumes position, hands carefully in place. "No, no, not like that, *mio amico,*" says Flavio, "Real captains use these," he says, pointing to his bare feet.

Flavio shows James how to balance on the built-in swivel chair and to steer using toe-ankle coordination. The tiny seed of panic is taking root. It isn't comforting to see a twelve-year-old steer the boat with his feet, even if a part of me wants to try it for myself. I check on Emma yet again. Just to make sure.

Yes. Lights out.

"Flavio, is this really necessary?" asks Sherry.

"Mom, please, let me do this," says James.

"Yes, *Mama*," says the captain, "let him do it. He is clever, strong boy."

Sherry looks at Keith. Keith looks at Sherry. They are cornered. "Fine" says Sherry, "but you must be nearby."

Why does no one ask me if I want a twelve-year-old to captain this ship? Why doesn't Flavio take my thoughts into consideration? I think to myself. I am surprised by my own extreme and irregular reaction. What is this feeling of panic and fear? Where is it coming from? If I were James, I would love to do this. Forget that. What about me? I am Jay. This is the kind of thing that I would love to do.

"Yes, yes, fine. I am not going nowhere," Flavio laughs reassuringly.

"Great! Yes! Thanks!" says James, and adeptly balances on the chair in front of the rudder, and steers the boat with his right foot.

Flavio also resumes his position, perching precariously between boat and sea. His left hand holds the side rail of the boat, his right hand raised in the air, a beacon for James to see. He sprawls towards the tanning girls, "Yes, where were we? Nightclubs?" He gestures straight ahead with his right hand.

The girls roll over towards him. He continues: "In Amalfi, there's a good club. Nice music. I can meet you there." He gestures slightly left.

"What's nice music? Like the songs from your girlfriend, Claudine?" asks the more hostile bikini girl.

"When are you free?" Flavio asks, looking directly at Mozzarella, intentionally ignoring her angry friend. He gesticulates straight. James adjusts the boat slightly.

"I don't know," says Mozzarella coolly, playing hard-to-get, "maybe we just go by ourselves." She giggles and turns to her friend, "what do you say?" Her friend perks up, her spirits are temporarily raised.

"Maybe," says Flavio, "but I can help you get in, you know and protect you … some people can be … a bit *aggresivo*, no? I help you." He gestures left and then immediately right.

"I don't understand," yells James. "Right or left?"

About three hundred meters away, there is a cone in the water. It is half submerged in the water and cemented onto a large rocky pole.

"Flavio," I say, "there is an obstacle straight ahead." There is a shrill sound in my head, ringing like an alarm. Is this what Emma feels like when she faces one of her fears?

"*Bellissima*, I can take you tonight, no? I get you at your hotel?" Flavio doesn't hear me, or simply ignores me. He gestures left. "I come and get you with or without your *amica*, yes? Maybe she is tired? Maybe she got too much sun?"

"So left it is then," says James and steers the boat with his foot. Sherry and Keith look up, towards James and then towards Flavio. We all look at the cone. It is getting nearer and nearer. It doesn't look incredibly large, but perhaps the iceberg that sank the Titanic didn't either, at first glance. It appears to be around two hundred meters away.

"Maybe I bring a friend for *la tua amica*? *Ci*? I have a friend for your friend," Flavio says, gesturing straight ahead.

"Flabbier, I don't think I should go straight; there's something in the water," calls James.

"Flavio, the boy needs help," shrills Sherry.

"Now," says Keith. "Go now." Flavio continues to gesture straight ahead.

"Flabbier!" calls James.

"Go Flavio, go," I shout and turn instinctively to shield Emma from what seems to be an imminent collision. The French girls look up and see the obstacle getting nearer and nearer. They gasp.

Flavio ignores everyone, determined to get a final answer, his hand still in the air indicating a straight position. "So I come pick you up? At nine is OK?" he asks. The cone is about a hundred meters away.

"Go," yells Mozzarella.

"*Arrête! T'es un idiot*," yells her friend.

"James!" yells Sherry.

"Captain!" yells Keith.

Kerry and Simon, who are now in brace positions in their parents' arms are both yelping and screaming.

"Go now," I shout.

"Help me, someone!" yells James.

Grunts from the intoxicated Australians and silence from the sleeping Emma.

"OK, OK!" says Flavio, "*Nessun problema. Rimanete calmi*. No problem. Just everyone keep calm. OK. No problem."

He swings back over the side into the boat so that his entire body is now completely engaged and ready to take action. He grabs the rudder and sharply steers the boat to the left, pushing James aside in the process. James grabs onto the built-in couch, and holds on for dear life. The ship veers sharply against the turbulence and a large wave pours onto each and every one of us. Keith clutches Kerry, and Kerry screams in her father's arms. Sherry holds Simon so tight that he objects, "I can't breathe. You are squashing me."

"Yeah!" James shouts, "that was so cool!"

From the bottom of the boat, the Australians, who have finally managed to get to their feet since the beginning of the commotion, are thrown back down. They roll about until they stop in a tangled mess. I throw myself over an oblivious Emma. As for the captain, as he restores the course of the boat and manages to evade the cone obstacle in its path, his beloved bucket hat flies off and away into the sea, revealing a rather unruly, messy head of dreadlocks braided with beads the color of the Jamaican flag.

Retching and groaning can be heard from the puddle of Australians at the bottom of the boat.

"I think I punctured my prostate," says Dean.

"You don't even know what a prostate is," says his wife.

The other Australian couple just moan.

"Cool!" yells James.

"Do it again, let's do it again!" yells Simon.

"No!" Keith, Sherry and Kerry yell in unison.

"You idiot," yells Mozzarella's angry friend and lets off a healthy string of expletives in French, and then, bursting into laughter, she adds, "*Regarde ses cheveux!*" – look at his hair!"

"Do not come and pick me up," says Mozzarella turning her nose up at the skipper and his knotty mane. "We will be fine by ourselves," she finishes off and puts her arm around her friend's shoulder.

"Wow," says a soaking wet Emma, stretching out beneath me. I get off of her in slow motion. Shaking the water out of my hair and eyes, I sit up and take a deep breath. Emma slides up next to me and sniffs in the cool air. "I had the best sleep ever!" she says.

"Well, good morning to you," I say in response.

Emma

I woke up, calm and collected, and in a cool puddle of water. All around me was complete pandemonium, most of it directed at Flavio, who was getting the boat to slow down to an anchored stop, his wild soggy hair flapping into his eyes. Jay was leaning over me like my makeshift scarf-cabana. I stretched from head to toe, feeling the water drip over me and down my sides. Jay sat upright.

"Wow," I said sitting up. "I had the best sleep ever!" I looked all around me as the commotion continued. The family from the UK were split down the middle, with the parents and daughter yelling angrily and shaking their fists, and the boys in a state of clear over-excitement and glee. The bikini girls were yelling derisively at the captain, screaming and pointing, while wiping themselves down with their wet towels. Every few seconds, they took a break to stop yelling at the esteemed captain and turned to each other to yell some more in fast, angry French. Meanwhile, the Australians were staggering on the lower deck, still half-drunk but also fully angry at being rolled around like bowling balls against the sides of the boat.

"You idiot, you moron," said Bob to the captain.

"What you do that for mate?" asked Dean. "I need some more alcohol," he added as an afterthought.

As for their wives, Bob's Kayla got up clutching her stomach and said, "Oh boy, I think I am going to be sick again!" she staggered over to the side of the boat making awkward-sounding retching noises. Dean's lovely and inebriated wife Judy, still in a bit of a blur, raised her head from the floor of the boat and said, "That was awesome you guys, let's do it again!"

"Yay!" yelled the boys, "again, again!" cheered Simon. "That was wicked, Flabbier!" cheered James. As for Jay, he looked over at me, and said quite calmly: "Well, good morning to you!"

Jay

I haven't heard of mutiny on board a semi-private cruise ship, but I think we got quite close. Even with Dean complaining about his prostate, and Bob cussing and groaning and leaning over at half mast, it was very clear that they were a formidable pair, intent on knocking Flavio into next week. The French ladies were willing partners, Mozzarella because she felt duped, and her friend because she felt vindicated. As for the gentle family from the UK, they were now the angry family from the UK, with parents Keith and Sherry like a pair of lionesses ready to attack Flavio for trying to hurt their cubs. Emma looked around with bewilderment, "What is going on here?"

To his credit, Flavio, with the boat now anchored, was completely aware of the delicacy of his situation. He took charge and did everything he could to restore order. First he pulled out a spare hat from a cupboard of the boat and covered his unruly locks. Then he motioned everyone for silence and began to talk.

"My friends," he said, "We are here, in the beautiful sea. For such a group of *persone speciali* – special people, I have a special treat. This I don't do with everyone. Before you go back to your hotel and continue your vacation, we must celebrate and drink to *la dolce vita* – to a sweet life." He opened the fridge and pulled out Limoncello and wine. The Australians perked up and even Keith and Sherry welcomed the drink. For the kids, he pulled out cans of soda and juices of all sorts. "Can I try some wine, mom?" asked Kerry. "Not a chance," answered her father. "Now, everyone come and take a drink, or I pass to you, *ci*. And we stand on top of the boat and celebrate," said Flavio.

One by one the passengers came by the kitchenette and took a drink or two or three. Emma and I chose Limoncello shots, and we all made our way to the top of the boat. The island of Capri was already a spot in the distance, the sea a blanket of clear blue stretching endlessly and calmly.

We all stood on the top of the boat and raised our glasses. A chorus of: *Cheers, bottoms up, Salut* and *Cin Cin*, rang out loudly.

Once the drinks were downed, a still silence and a quiet calm enveloped the boat like a glowing aura. The chaos of just a few minutes earlier was quickly forgiven or forgotten. If it is possible for a group of seemingly unrelated and unfamiliar people to have an intimate moment of reconciliation and harmony, I think this is what we had. The four Australians, the family from the UK, the two French young women, me and Emma, led by our skipper Flavio, stepped forward in a spontaneous, warm group embrace. Once the moment was over, we took a step back. But our captain wasn't done quite yet. "And now," he announced in a loud voice, "now, we jump into the water." The quiet calm quickly became a confused calm. "Did you say jump?" asked Keith, "We are three meters above the water, and we could break a leg."

"Are we allowed to drink and jump?" asked Bob's wife, Judy, speech still slightly slurred.

"My bikini might just fall off," says Mozzarella, loudly. Comments were coming in fast and furious.

"Trying to off us in the middle of the sea, eh, mate?" said Bob, "smooth…"

"What ya talking about?" asked the macho Dean. "We could do this with our eyes closed and hands tied behind our backs."

"Wait a moment," said Kayla, his lovely wife, "come here and I will tie your hands." She and Judy laughed uproariously.

"No!" said Sherry, "no, no, no."

"Please, please, please?" said the kids.

I too gave the idea some thought, mainly wondering what *"Death by"* scenarios Emma was currently playing in her head. I turned to her. Emma looked at me, said not a word, grabbed my hand and squeezed it tight, let my hand go, pulled her hair out of her hair band and flung her head back, so that her hair was released like a flowing mane. She threw her shot glass high into the sky and over the clear water, where it landed with a gentle plop. The group, silenced once again, watched the glass fly over the side of the boat, their heads following the motion of the hurtling and spinning object. Then, without a second of deliberation or hesitation, Emma stepped over to the edge of the boat, and without looking back, dove over the side – *"La Sir-Emma Serena,"* like a serene mermaid.

Emma

Without a moment of hesitation, or trepidation or fear, I dove over the side of the boat and into the water. Like Alice down the rabbit hole, I jumped without thinking of rhyme or reason, impact or consequence. I didn't stop to analyze, calculate or run through *Death by* scenarios. I didn't try to do risk analysis and mitigation. I didn't consider probabilities or statistics or precedents. I didn't look for verification, validation, assurance, approval or encouragement. I didn't weigh the pros and cons. I didn't look left and right. I just did it.

It was not an elegant, lady-like jump. It was a bomb of a dive. I exploded into the water, causing a massive eruption of blue-green spray that broke in the air and onto the side of the boat. It was a belly-flop of a dive with my stomach hitting first, and then my chin, my arms and my hands, followed by my legs and feet, which were soon submerged. I broke the water with a resounding and reverberating bang. It was a sound that entered my body like an electric shock and then disappeared. It simply evaporated. I could feel the tingling and pain of the impact, and it made me feel alive. The sound of my body clashing and colliding with millions of water molecules was quickly replaced by a silence that was heavy, intense and dense. It became even more so as I burrowed deeper, and deeper into the water. I could feel the silence within me as sure as I could feel the beating of my heart. Around me, I could see rays of light causing a kaleidoscope of different colors. I could feel different currents washing over and around me, some cool, some cold and some warm. I could see particles of rock and shell, and bits of kelp and plant life floating and bobbing around. Fish darted in all directions, trying to reestablish their schools, broken by my dive. I could make out the floor of the sea, a pebbled and shelly bed in parts, and in other parts rocky and green. I went down as far as I could, stretching my body to its limit until it began to resist and to demand oxygen. Then, like an arrow, smooth and sharp, I shot up to the surface face-first, releasing thousands of air bubbles from my nose and mouth. The bubbles floated with me to the top of the water. As I soared to the surface, the water became less dense, less dark. The light became clearer, brighter and more translucent. I exploded out of the water and gasped for air. As a wave of oxygen replenished my lungs, the silhouette that I could see as I was breaking through the surface of the water crystallized, and from an ambiguous fuzzy mass, I now recognized five Brits, four Australians, two Frenchwomen, one Italian and one Jay, watching and waiting for me, from where I had left them at the top of the boat. They were looking expectantly at the water, like spectators at an opera, intensely staring at center stage, waiting for the fat lady to sing. I shook the water out my eyes and hair, and started to tread water, making large circular motions with my hands and legs: doing slow and strong strokes. "Well," I said, "what are you waiting for, come on in already. Just jump!"

Jay

I did not expect Emma to jump. In the few seconds between Flavio's suggestion and her spontaneous dive, I was running a few scenarios of my own, considering what would be the very best and easiest way to get Emma into the water. One way or the other, I was determined that it would happen. Should I jump first so that she can see it can be done? Should I let her see the others go in first and let the pressure of the group work its magic? Should I convince, coax, or even seduce her to jump with me, telling her how brave and determined, daring and sexy she is? Should I remind her that this is a time to test limits, to shake and rattle the *status quo* as if it never were? Should I remind her of the fears that she has already faced: the dark subterranean tunnels of Napoli, the Chinese filled minivan, climbing an active volcano, the precarious corner and cliffs of the Amalfi coast, the sea bus filled with regular people, breathing, eating and just living. And then, she jumped!

It was the most beautiful, most elegant thing I ever saw. I stepped over to the side of the boat. I saw her enter the water and disappear. I briefly wondered if, like a mermaid, she would simply swim away and join the watery underworld. I watched as the ripples disappeared and the surface of the water became completely opaque again, as if there had never been a disturbance. The others joined me, peering over the edge.

"Mom, do you think that she will be OK?" asked James.

"Sure honey, she will be just fine," said Sherry in a nervous voice, and to her husband, she whispered a bit too loudly, "Do you think this is a good idea so close to her surgery?" Keith just shrugged, his eyes transfixed on the water.

"Yes, moron, he will be fine," said Kerry to James. Little Simon was hanging onto her leg. "Get off me already, Simon."

"Don't call your brother a moron," said Sherry automatically

"Well, fuck me," said the ever-eloquent Bob.

"I didn't see that coming," said Kayla. "Still waters run deep."

"I think we need more alcohol," said Dean, shaking his shot glass in his right hand, as if he had just remembered that it was empty.

"That's for sure!" said Judy. "It's definitely time for a refill."

"I'm scared," said Mozzarella, clutching onto Flavio's hand quite unexpectedly. "Where is she? *Mon dieu.*"

Flavio pulled her close, seizing his opportunity to regain lost ground.

"*Salope*," said Mozzarella's friend – *Bitch!* she said, not really committing as to whether she was referring to the on-again flirtation of her friend now clinging to Flavio like wet glue, or to Emma, the new center of everyone else's attention.

"*Bravissima, auguri*" shouted Flavio: sending encouraging words of congratulations to Emma, who was still underwater and couldn't hear them at all. He held his princess tight and peered over the side of the boat. Notwithstanding his enthusiasm, I am quite sure that he was anxious to see Emma alive and kicking and above the watery surface. I am not sure what the Italian word is for *liability*, but I reckon that he was trying to recall his insurance policy in the few seconds that it took for Emma to resurface.

At first we saw a few air bubbles. And then the few air bubbles became a thousand bubbles, and then her hands emerged, thumb to thumb, sharp and tight. Her hands made small ripples in the water. The small ripples became big ripples until the surface of the water was covered with hundreds of expanding, concentric circles. They got bigger and bigger until they broke on the edge of the boat. First emerged the hands, and then the arms and then came Emma's head. She came out like a newborn, gasping for a breath, taking oxygen into her lungs for the very first time. She wiped the water from her eyes and mouth. She shook her hair out and looked up at us. "Well," she said, "What are you waiting for? Come on in already. Just jump!"

Emma

I am treading water, watching the others enter the sea one way or another. The water is a perfect playground. There is a lot of laughter and happy movement. I look around me and see moments and memories being formed. If I had a giant butterfly net, I would swoop over from above and capture the moment. I would place it in a glass jar and keep it on my desk. Whenever I am blue or down, or lacking perspective, I would shake it like one of those glass snow globes. And when I would do that, the boat would rock and rise in the water, the people would jump, or float or swim. The perfect waters would wash over the happy figurines.

Jay and I would also be in the jar. In my vision, we are two tiny figurines submerged deep in the blue. We take turns diving to the depths. Each dive brings us closer to the sandy bed of the sea. There, amongst the shells and sea foliage, is a shiny treasure waiting just for us. It is a shot glass. It sparkles and glistens. It conjures up images of yellow, lemony sunlight. It is ours for the taking, provided that we have the necessary stamina, perseverance, and oxygen. It is ours for the taking, as a challenge, and as a reminder of many moments of perfection captured in glass.

Jay

I am not sure who broke the spell. But within minutes, I was the last man standing on deck.

I watched as Kerry grabbed her brother James, "Come on moron, we're going in." They held hands and took off, crying out all the way down.

"*Geee ron iiii-mo,*" screamed Kerry.

"*Tiiiiim-berrr,*" yelled James.

Sherry, caught up in the movement of her two embracing teens, was so moved by their unity that tears welled up in her eyes. "Look Keith," she gushed, "our babies are growing up."

Overwhelmed with emotion and what looked like a visceral need to be near her kids, she took little Simon by the hand and said "We are going to James and Kerry, what do you say Simon? Are you ready to jump with me?"

"Yes, jump. Let's jump," said Simon. Before Sherry could count down from three, he let go of her hands and flew like a kamikaze into the water. "Simon, wait, Simon, I'm coming…" called Sherry and jumped in right after him.

"Simon, wait, you forgot your arm bands!" shouted Keith. Simon landed in the water with a bang. He came up from under the water, gasping and spluttering, his eyes shining and bright. Once Keith saw him, he threw the tricolor-decorated inflatable armbands over the side of the boat urgently in Simon's direction. They floated down nonchalantly, riding the gentle breeze, landing way out of Simon's range.

"Simon, I'll get you," shouted Kerry and with big strokes swam towards her little brother.

"Go Simon! You did it," shouted James and he swam towards the armbands. Kerry and James caught up with Simon and helped him to gain his balance and his breath. Within seconds, Sherry joined the group and they formed a neat family circle, without a nervous-looking Keith.

"Come on Keith, jump, jump!" shouted Sherry at her husband.

"Come on, Dad," shouted Kerry.

"Don't be chicken," shouted James, "Get in the water!"

"Jump!" said Simon "It's not scary."

"No," Keith shouted back, "I think I will just wait here, you know. Someone has to watch our things."

I wasn't the only one watching the kids fly into the water. Dean and Judy, Australian couple number one, watched as the kids jumped in. "Oh look," said Judy, "maybe we should have brought the kids too, look how much fun these guys are having. Come and see, they are playing in the water. It's so adorable." She wobbled perilously close to the edge of the boat. Her entry into the water was not completely intentional; truth is; she was just a bit too drunk to make the decision consciously. As she wobbled over to the side of the boat to get a better view of the kids bobbing around in the water, she unwittingly slipped over the side. She looked up at her husband as she was falling and shouted up at him *"bbbbyyye,"* too drunk to care. Her husband, Dean, a bit intoxicated himself, couldn't stop laughing as she fell. "Judy," he laughed, "are you OK?" He was doubled over with laughter. Bob and Kayla, Australian couple number two, watched Dean as he laughed. "Don't be such an ass, Dean," said Kayla, "go help your wife before she drowns." When the laughing Dean showed no signs of jumping in, Kayla took matters into her own hands and swiftly pushed him over the side. Dean went flying over the side, his arms and legs swinging in every direction, only just missing Judy as he hit the water. "Ow," he said, "I think I busted my prostate."

"You silly bugger," said Judy, "you don't even know what a prostate is." They splashed each other in the water. It occurred to me that I was not really sure what a prostate is either. Emma would know. Emma would *definitely* know.

I looked out to the water. Emma was still swimming in large, slow circles. Her head was above the water.

She watched me as she glided around in the water. She was so beautiful. The Australians broke my focus. "Well Kayla," said Bob, "I am impressed, you got the bastard. And now I am going to get you." He charged Kayla, picked her up and the two of them went plunging together over the side of the boat, screaming with laughter on their way down.

Meanwhile, I could see that Sherry and the kids were still trying to persuade Keith to jump into the water. It made me think about the many times that I have tried to persuade, coax, cajole and even manipulate Emma into doing something that scares her to her inner core.

"Dad, we want you here with us," yelled Kerry.

"I can come down from the other side," said Keith.

"You can," said James, "but where would the fun be in that?"

"Honey," said Sherry, "really it's OK. You can do it. Our things can stay as they are. Nothing will happen to them."

"Come on, Dad," said Simon, "please, you can have my armbands!"

"Oh, all right then," said Keith. He took a couple of steps back in order to gather some speed. He inhaled deeply and then exhaled, making a deep whistling sound, and began to run.

"Yeah!" cheered the kids, watching their father build up momentum in preparation for a dramatic dive. "Go Dad!"

As Keith ran forward, he slipped on a puddle of water on the top of the boat. Suddenly, he disappeared from the sight of the kids and Sherry in the water. He landed with a smack on his backside in the middle of the puddle. I grimaced and thought to myself. *Ouch.* That definitely must have hurt.

"Owww!" he groaned.

"Dad," yelled the kids.

"Keith, are you OK?" called Sherry, "Keith?"

I turned to see how he was doing. He was untangling himself from a contorted mess on the floor. "Owww!" he groaned again, rubbing his stinging backside. I offered him a hand, which he took readily. "He's fine," I shouted back at the family.

Keith lifted his aching backside out of the puddle, picked himself up. "I am fine," he confirmed.

"Come in, Dad, come in," shouted Simon.

"What the hell," Keith said. He closed his eyes for a few seconds as if he was praying silently. He took a deep breath, muttered "Take two," under his breath, and jumped into the water.

"Go Dad! Yeah! Yes, Keith!" shouted his family as he joined them with a resounding splash in the sea.

The way I see it, Flavio really should have been concerned with all the goings on: minors jumping in without their parents, adults jumping in half-inebriated, some being pushed, some being dragged. Passengers slipping on puddles and injuring their hind parts. But the truth was, from where I was standing, I could see that he was caught up in an awkward triangle. His beloved Mozzarella was still holding on to him. Her angry-faced friend was still glaring at him, and the two were bickering between them. It looked to me like it would have been very easy for our skipper Flavio to persuade Mozzarella to jump in the water with him; she was like putty in his hand at this point. Then again, perhaps he was thinking that it would be more satisfying for him to simply push both of them and to watch them go down together. I am definitely all for living for the moment, but he was still the captain. The safety of his passengers should be paramount, more important even than his own enjoyment. Besides which, he was a young man, there would be other seas to sail, and other tourists the color of soft white cheese. He did not disappoint me. *"Le mie belle signore,* my beautiful ladies. Why fight? You have come here to have fun. You are best friends – no? Friends should have fun together – no? You hold her hand," he took Mozzarella's hand from his. Mozzarella took her friend's hand. "That's good, that's friends. That's how we do it." The two girls faced each other, holding hands.

"Je suis désolé, j'étais juste un peu jalouse" – I'm sorry, I was just a bit jealous! said the one girl to her best friend and travel companion.

"Je suis désolé, je n'aurais pas dû laisser un mec nous séparer." – I'm sorry, I should never have let a boy get between us! responded her best friend and the center of Flavio's attention.

"It's OK," said the one.

"It's all right," said the other.

The girls made up with a big warm hug.

"I happy now," said the gallant skipper. "It is good that you are friends." He paused for a few seconds and looked intensely at the girls in their tight embrace. Then he said, *"Adesso,* and now that you friends again, we jump to water together."

He intercepted their hug, getting once more in the middle of the friendship. He held each girl in one arm, and charged with them to the edge of the boat. Together, the threesome flew over the side and into the water.

So there I was, last man standing on the top of the boat, watching the others jump in one after the other, while I stood still and calm like that statue of the Immaculate Virgin on top of the obelisk back in *San Domenico Maggiore* square in Naples. I was watching the world happen around me, frozen in time, and frozen in motion. Emma, in the meantime, was still treading water endlessly in the sea, not taking her eyes off of me for a minute. She waited patiently, without saying a word. Her circular movements broke the spell, unfroze my arms and legs from their atrophied marble state. "I am coming Emma," I yelled, and dove into the water, swimming straight into Emma's embrace.

My wish is to stay always like this,
living quietly in a corner of nature.

Claude Monet

Emma

I am on my back staring at the blue sky. Tiny wispy clouds flit by like pearls rolling on a freshly polished floor. My eyes watch them, mesmerized. Jay is next to me. I can hear his breathing, deep and calm. I can't tell if his eyes are open or closed, but I can tell that he is happy and content. Behind me, Flavio, our young skipper, is back at the rudder. On either side of him are the lovely bikini girls. I can hear the three of them discussing evening plans. Maybe dinner? Maybe dancing? Definitely together. Flavio lets them take turns steering the boat. The girls are generous in letting each other take turns. Flavio remains focused on the sea, while at the same time, tries to work out the logistics of the evening up ahead which will open a whole new chapter of this chance encounter.

Just in front of where Jay and I are stretched out in the sun, Sherry, Keith and the kids are all recalling the events of the past few hours and laughing.

"Did you see me jump, Dad?" says Simon, "I did it all by myself and I wasn't even scared like you." The older kids giggled. "Yes, you did," says Keith. "You were more brave than me. And your jump was better than mine, little man."

"That's for sure," interjects Sherry. "One minute you were there and then you were gone. It was like a magic trick."

"It was hysterical," says Kerry. "Really hilarious, Dad. Pity we didn't film it."

"Yes," says James, "especially the sound of you going *owwww!*"

"Maybe it was funny for the likes of you," says Keith, "but I am going to be stiff for a week. I think my behind is black and blue. Want to see?" he says, stretching at an angle making as if he is about to show them his butt.

"No, Daddy no!" yells Kerry.

"Disgusting," says James.

"I want to see, let's see!" says Simon.

Sherry and Keith laugh and laugh.

As for the Australians, they too are in various stages of relaxation and recollection. The loud voices of the two boisterous couples carry all the way above the whirring boat engine and the rolling and spraying waters of the sea.

"I can't believe that you pushed me in, Kay," says Dean, "I am going to get you when you least expect it – *so go to sleep with your eyes open*," he says in a deep, ominous voice.

"If you want to get my wife, you will have to go through me first," says a chivalrous Bob.

"Yes, me too Dean," says Judy to her husband, "Kayla was protecting my honor," and she blows a kiss to her long-time friend.

"Oh well," says Dean. "Going through the both of you to get my revenge on Kayla – now that sounds like a challenge. I'll drink to that," and he starts to refill all the shot glasses. "Actually mate, the way I see it, you will drink to pretty much anything." says Bob. "That's true," says Dean. Everyone laughs. "Cheers to that," Dean adds and they all raise their glasses, clink them together, and down the drops of the acidic sweet lemony liqueur. Although I am not with them, I imagine the lemony taste going through me, leaving a healing and soothing trail of tingling warmth. It makes me feel magical and new. I think if you could see me from the inside, my body would be aglow with a thousand rays of gentle, yellow sunshine. I turn to Jay. "You know," I say, "I never did thank you for bringing me here."

"Thank me? What for?" asks Jay, "I knew all along that you would love it!"

"Liar." I say and laugh.

He laughs as well. "OK," he continues, "It took a bit of time, but I knew you would love it – *eventually*."

Jay

We're packing up. Our clothes are laid out on the bed. Emma has a system: clean clothes on the bottom and dirty clothes on the top. This optimizes the unpacking and clean-up process when we land back at home. I have our case on the bed, and am staring at it as if it were some foreign object. Emma helps me gather all of our things, and then she announces that she is letting me take over from here. It would feel like an honor and a privilege, if I didn't hate packing so much. But I guess this is part of Emma's journey. So I try to stick with Emma's unwritten but unshakeable guidelines, take a deep breath and begin. First the big items: pants, dresses, shirts. I shake them out until I hear the material whip, releasing all dust and ironing out all creases. Then I fold.

Each item has its procedure: shirts in a particular way, especially those with collars, and dresses in another way. I put shoes in shoe bags or plastic bags and stick them in the corners of the case. I fit the smaller items into the smaller nooks and crevices that are formed by the spaces in the other clothes. I wonder what to do with the oil lamp.

I consider leaving it with Stefano to add to his inventory of this lovely little villa alongside the crockery, cutlery and complimentary condiments but then I decide to pack it.

On the other hand, I throw all of the remaining surgical masks slam-dunk in the waste basket. This is the price that Emma must pay for leaving the packing in my hands. Next, I pack a green canvas tarp, specifically packed by Emma because of its size and water resilient nature. This will be the separator between the clean clothes and the dirty ones. Then I begin again, this time including the towels, Emma's beach scarf or makeshift cabana, our swim gear and hats and all the other clothes that have seen better days, including the shirt from Pompeii and the two shirts from Vesuvius.

I work with a methodological rhythm, finding some kind of comfort in the mindlessness of the activity. I talk to myself aloud through the process methodologically and carefully: "Sort clean to dirty. Pack clean items first. Sort clean items from largest to smallest. Now, pack in descending order. Pack items of awkward shapes after the big items, but before the small items. Wrap them up depending on the nature of the piece. Use the smaller items to fill the open spaces. Cover up the clean items using the tarp. Now, start the whole process again."

I can see why this method is engaging. There is a pleasing sense of order in packing according to Emma's gospel. I could definitely get used to this.

Emma

I can't believe that this is the last day before we travel. I am supposed to be packing, but I have got an inexplicable urge to go down to the beach one last time. I think Jay would have liked to have come with me, but today he is the time-keeper, or the guardian of the clock, and he has taken it upon himself to make sure that we leave enough time to get back to the airport in Naples.

We have agreed that he will call me if he sees that I am running late or I lose track of time. He is at the villa, sorting, packing and counting down time. I have gone out to wander in the open air.

I am actually kind of pleased to have this time to myself. I am half way down the stairs, the mountains behind me, the valley on either side, thinking about how the vegetation here reaches out to the sea. The fig trees are contorted and bent. The lemon trees are gnarled and twisted, their branches, like hands, stretch out as far as they can in order to try and let even the smallest twiggy finger dip in the water. Why *wouldn't* they be this way? I can feel it too from where I stand. This sea is like a magnet, everything leads, leans, and stretches towards it. Even the ginger cat, sleeping on the stairs of the church, is lying perpendicular to the step so that it can look towards the endless sea.

Here I am, walking step-by-step, each gait getting nearer and nearer the water. I make it through the narrow, twisted stairways. I walk down the windy paths through the ancient houses with their balconies adorned with flower boxes and shrines. I walk through the ancient passageway that has protected the city throughout the ages and I come face-to-face with the sea.

I sit down at the first place I see and order an espresso and a dessert, whatever fruit is available. The waitress is a young woman. Probably the daughter of the owner, who is herself wiping down the menus in preparation for the start of a new day.

"*Grazie*," I say to the young woman as she brings me my order.

"*Prego*" she answers, "it is my pleasure."

The girl turns to go.

"Excuse me, may I ask you a question?" I ask her.

She turns back towards me. "*Ci*," she says politely, "*certo*," –certainly.

"What's it like here when the summer season is over and the people are gone?"

She turns back at me, ponders for a few seconds and then answers. "Well, there are almost always tourists here," she says. "Sometimes there are a lot of people and sometimes there are less. When there are less, we simply continue doing things, but much more slowly," she answers with a smile. She is about to walk away, but then she adds, "But you know, Atrani is like…it's like a stone on the road, you know, it is so small, you can go through it without stopping. You can pass it without realizing you were here."

I think back to the day that we arrived and the angry conversation with the travel agent trying to explain via descriptions of landmarks and road signs how to meet up with our guide, Stefano. "So, what makes you stay here?" I ask, "a young woman like yourself? Surely you want to explore the world and meet people and be in a big city?"

"Well," she says with a smile, "I do go out. I have lived in other places and will go back to *Roma* soon to continue my studies, but this is my home. My mother is here and I will live here."

She takes a break from talking and looks at me intently. "For me, leaving Atrani is a bit like travelling, you know, a bit like being a tourist. I go out to see the world that is out there. I also go to remind me about where I belong, where is my home."

"I can understand that," I tell her, "*grazie*." The young woman, so self-assured, walks away to bus the next table or to her mother, or to the next thing she knows that she needs to do. She will continue to do this season and the next, and the next. She isn't in a constant quest to validate her choices. Nor does she fear the unknown that she will inevitably encounter in this place or the next. She doesn't need to use travel as shock therapy in order to stabilize the *status quo*. I stare at her in awe and with a deep sense of gratitude.

I pull out my mobile phone and dial the international code. A few little digits and then a few more. The phone begins to ring. It rings about seven times until she picks up.

"Emmy, Emmy is that you? Are you OK? You are not scheduled to call today. Is everything OK? Has there been an accident? Is it Jay? Is it you? Oh god, I knew this was a bad day."

"Mom, Mom, stop a minute, stop. Just give me a chance..." I interrupt her.

"I told Jackie that no good would come from this trip. This travel thing that you do, it just upsets everything. It turns everything upside down. And to what end? For a few pictures that my eyes can't see? So that dogs can get sick and die?"

"Mom, please, take a breath. Everything is fine. Really, everything is fine." I say.

"Are you sure, you are not lying to spare my feelings? I may be sick and I am probably dying, but I can handle it. You can tell me. I can't have secrets from my children," she says.

"Mom, everything is OK. Everything is better than OK. In fact, I am feeling great."

"Really," she says with a suspicious voice. "What do you mean?"

"Well Mom," I say, "I just called to say that I am having a lovely time in Italy and I miss you and I'm excited to be coming home." There is complete silence on the line. For four seconds, then another five seconds, then another three. "Mom," I say, "hello, have I lost you? Are you there? Hello, hello?" I say to the empty line.

"Emmy, just tell me straight, am I dying, is this what this call is about?" she asks.

I laugh, "No Mom, you are not dying. I have just come to a realization that I have been too hard on myself, too involved with being scared and needing routine. I have come to understand that I need to let go a bit and let the world in. So that's what I am doing." My words are greeted with silence on the line. "I love you Mom. I will see you when I get back. OK?"

"OK," she says after a few minutes. More silence ensues. "Are you sure I am not dying?" she asks again.

I laugh, "Mom, I called to say that everything will be OK. Send my love to Jackie. Bye."

"Bye," she said, too speechless to add anything else.

I leave money to pay for my order and then get up. I walk along the beach until I get to the water. I take off my shoes. It isn't a hot day, but there are people in the water nonetheless. I hike up my skirt as far as it can go and wade right in. When I get in as deep as I can without getting my clothes wet, I turn around. With my back facing the sea, my gaze directly towards the Atrani valley and the rugged mountain top, I search for our little hideaway villa, with no real luck. I take a deep breath and try to seal the moment in my memory so that I can conjure it up whenever I want to. I start to make my way back out the water. I pick up my shoes from where I left them, fish my mobile phone from my handbag, and make one last phone call.

"Hey, Babe," I say when Jay answers the phone. "How's it going?"

"Just fine," he says, I think you will be proud of me. I definitely feel like I have got the hang of this packing thing. I might just take it over from you…for our next trip."

"I have created a monster," I say, laughing, "well, just continue as you are, I have one more thing that I need to do and then I am on my way home. Is that OK?"

"It sure is," says Jay. "Either way, I still have quite a bit to do here."

"OK," I say, "I will make it fast." And we both hang up. I leave the sandy beach and start walking towards Amalfi.

Jay

Emma comes back with a huge smile on her face. She is tanned, rested and relaxed. She hands me a shopping bag with two narrow boxes. "Sorry to do this after all your hard work, but is there room for one more thing? I figured we should bring some Italy back with us. It is Limoncello."

"Good idea. I will squeeze it in. I am sure that we can find some room," I say, thinking of the oil lamp. "Wow, you really went to town here; there is a lot of glass I can hear clanking around." Emma just smiles.

I open the trunk of the car, unzip the case and feel around with my hands until I find the oil lamp. I gently extract it from its warm nest, hand it to Emma, who hands me the boxes in return. I slip the boxes into the open space, and make every effort to cushion the boxes with extra clothes and support.

"That should do it," I say. Then I cover it up, lock the case, slam the trunk shut and we are ready to go. Stefano waves to us from the entrance of the villa. Emma goes up to him to thank him for the stay. I wonder briefly whether she is giving him the more accurate stair count, or whether she has decided to keep that information to herself. Regardless, she hands him the oil lamp and he gives her a quick hug. We are ready to leave the villa behind. Emma gets into the passenger side, and I squat into the driver's seat.

"Hey," she says, "before I sit down, do you want me to drive?"

I laugh at her. "Baby steps Emma, baby steps." She laughs too and I start the engine. The car wheezes and groans and complains all the way up the narrow driveway.

Emma

It has been two months since we came back home. Two months is just the right amount of time to get back into the swing of things, to restore the smooth running of the household, to get the body back in sync with the day-to-day routine. But the truth is, things are not the same as they were before. For one thing, I haven't replenished my supply of surgical masks. Nor do I buy garlic anymore. I can't stand the sight or smell of it at all. My morning routine no longer consists of stretching and breathing, but rather, I leave the house together with Jay and we go for a jog around the block. After that, we come home, shower, he goes to work and I start my day after fifteen minutes of meditation. Sometimes I succeed and sometimes I don't. I find that it really helps me to focus on an object that conjures up a memory of something that relaxes me and puts me at ease.

So I have carved out a little corner for us at home. It feels a bit like a magical cave. I have thrown pillows on the floor and draped my scarf that used to be a makeshift cabana on top. Jay placed the picture that Lucia gave him of *La Sirena Serena* for me to look at. He has added some more pictures over time, pictures that Lucia has sent him of her work as it has evolved. The mermaid is now almost fully grown and mature. She has long wavy fern hair interwoven with flowers and fronds. She is diving into the water, and the water is a very real pond with water lilies and reeds. I can almost imagine the sounds of frogs and fish and air bubbles popping, and dragonflies buzzing and snapping by. The homely corner looks a bit like one of those shrines in the doorways of Atrani.

Our day often begins and ends in this space. The object that most soothes and relaxes me, the centerpiece of my little shrine, is a plate of glass lemons that I purchased that last day when I was alone in Amalfi. The perfection of the glass lemons takes my breath away. I focus on them and I close my eyes. I imagine the lemon tree groves in the Atrani valley swaying gently in the breeze, heavy with fruit and constantly leaning towards the blue-green sea. I can smell the citrus in the air, gentle and strong at the same time. I can taste the Limoncello, tart and sweet on the tongue. A taste that shakes me up and wakes me up, and makes me all warm and fuzzy inside.

I have decided that this little gentle corner will house all of our treasures from our travels. We are already considering where we should go to next. Jay insists that it is my turn to choose. I have no idea where to begin. Maybe we can go and visit Changming in Shanghai? I've never been to Berlin; maybe we could give Frauke and Jürgen a call? How about Sidney; Australia sounds like it could be fun. Maybe that is an option? Jay and I know a couple of experienced sailors who could show us around. The world is such a place of limitless possibility.

Jay

I try to imagine her that day in Amalfi. I can see her walking with determination on the side of the road. There is no space for pedestrians, so you have to take your chances walking alongside cars and motorbikes, minivans and buses. I am sure that Emma stared down many a driver who came a bit too close for her liking. On the other hand, with traffic on her right and the sea on her left, maybe she walked staring at the crystal water, mesmerized and hypnotized by the blue-green swirls. Did she notice the crowds in Amalfi? Did she see the tourists, the locals, the people passing through? Did she have a moment of regret, or claustrophobia, and look for a dark corner to catch her breath? Or, did she stop to help a family looking for an on-the-spot photographer willing to capture them through the lens of a mobile phone camera? Did she engage with a street performer singing opera on the side of the street? Or, did she stop to buy a bottle of water from a little side kiosk filled with cigarette smoke and the sound of a soccer match blaring from the ancient television set? And when she came up to that shop at the center of the Amalfi pedestrian mall, did she hesitate before she stepped inside?

Did she look at the glass lemons from the window and say to herself, "You can do this Emma!" or did she just march in and say to the salesperson, "I want those lemons; pack them up carefully because they have a long journey to make." Did she think to herself, *I want these glass lemons, because they have meaning to me,* or did she say *I am allowed to be frivolous and silly and buy something decorative that has no other significance but to make me happy*? Perhaps she said to herself, *I am getting these for Jay, because he will like them.* I have no idea, and I haven't asked her. Maybe one day she will tell me.

I can picture her leaving the shop, excited and victorious, imagining my face as I unwrap the surprise. I am sure that she left the center of Amalfi hugging the box of wrapped glass lemons, and another box of bottled Limoncello that she purchased to complete the illusion, to fortify the smoke screen, so that the surprise would remain intact. I am sure that she practically ran up the three hundred and fourteen and a half stairs to get back to the villa. And when she reached me, the suitcase already packed, I can imagine her fighting back the urge to tell me what she had done, to share her adventure. It must have taken all of her effort to crack only a gentle smile and to say: "Sorry to do this after all your hard work, but is there room for one more thing? I figured we should bring some Italy back with us. It is Limoncello."

Acknowledgements

Some things in life are as a result of careful consideration and calculation. This book definitely wasn't. I assure you all, it was quite accidental. Nevertheless, it came into being because of three special people who set the ball in motion:

Firstly, my mother, *Arleen Leon Kaplinski* who inadvertently kick-started a thought process and a stream of consciousness, as my family and I were vacationing on the Amalfi coast. Secondly, my husband, *Alessandro Mayer*, who played along with me, not quite expecting that I would write it all down. Thirdly, my friend, *Keren Okman*, who introduced me to NaNoWriMo, and convinced me to give it a shot.

I would like to acknowledge my first readers, my parents, *Solly* and *Arleen*, and my sisters, *Tali* and *Carmi*. Your encouragement and enthusiasm was contagious. I humbly hope that I deserve it.

To my friend and editor, *Judy Kestecher*. Who knew that ten years later we would start a new journey together?

For help with translation, *Alessandro Mayer* and *Linda Fenlon*. There is still no substitute for real people who *live* languages.

To NaNoWriMo, that significant platform which provided the framework I needed to transform resolutions to actions. I am grateful for all that you do. If you, dear reader, have come this far and are considering whether or not to see if you can take your love for reading, writing, creativity and imagination to the next level, I encourage you all to visit /nanowrimo.org/.

References

Partial quote from "O sole mio". Lyrics by Giovanni Capurro. Music by Eduardo di Capua.

www.ingramcontent.com/pod-product-compliance
Lightning Source LLC
Chambersburg PA
CBHW051113160726
47998CB00026B/321